# The Cabin on Ghostly Pond

# The Cabin on Ghostly Pond

BY MARJORIE REYNOLDS

*Pictures by* **LORENCE BJORKLUND**

HARPER & ROW · PUBLISHERS · NEW YORK AND EVANSTON

C.1

# THE CABIN ON GHOSTLY POND

Library of Congress catalog card number: 62-7943

For Roger

# The Cabin on Ghostly Pond

# 1

The dreary March day was drawing to a close. From a hotel room window high on the tenth floor, Jo watched lights come on in city buildings and then saw neon signs blink into brightness. One advertised a soft drink. On his last birthday Jo had asked for and received a whole case of it from his father. Jo's father had always been ready to give him presents, expensive ones. But Jo would rather his father had taken him camping or sailing, or even just gone walking with him.

Jo flattened his freckled nose against the cold glass of the window. Slow, oily looking drops of rain drained down the pane. If he looked at them closely he became rather cross-eyed, and the effect was interesting. There was a heavy dullness inside him that was not just boredom, or even indigestion. Perhaps it came from missing his father, who had been divorced from his mother a month before. Living in a hotel was awful, Jo decided; although where they had lived before hadn't been any too wonderful either. There hadn't been any place to play ball, and anyway there had been no other boys on the street, only girls and a baby in a carriage that might be a boy someday.

His mother had been so particular about the house that it spoiled living there. She was forever saying, "Be careful of the flowers, Jo, don't throw your basketball here; pick up your stuff, Jo, and put everything away—we're having people in and I want the place neat. Don't ride your bike in the driveway, Jo, people are coming. Why don't you go up to your room and watch television?"

It seemed to Jo as if that was the way it always was. Always he was in the way. If he tried to do something nice to please her, it always turned out wrong. One time, just before the guests arrived, he had carried a trayful of glasses to the porch of their ranch house and had tripped on the sill. His mother had slapped him, and when he tried to pick up the broken glass, he had cut his hand and got blood all over her new dress.

Right now in some house or club his mother was probably laughing and talking to crowds of people. As she left the hotel an hour before she had kissed him absent-mindedly on the forehead and said, "I'll ask them to send you up a chicken sandwich and some ice cream. I probably won't be late, but if I am, just go to bed when you want to." And the door closed and she was gone.

Now the city lights were shining through a mist of rain. Down in the street below Jo could imagine the wet splashing of car tires. Perhaps even now a taxi was stopping in front of the hotel, bringing his mother home. But in his heart he knew it wasn't so.

Jo turned from the window and sat down. He lit the reading light and pulled a large book from the table onto his lap.

You might call it a book of dreams. Anyway, Jo had made it himself, with pictures cut from magazines. The first pages were about a boat, a neat little craft with light oars. Carefully lettered on the next page was the caption *Where I Go In My Boat*. Then followed pictures of lakes and rivers, beautiful and mysterious.

Jo turned the pages slowly. The hotel room faded away, and he could hear the dip of the oars, feel the pull on his back muscles. Mountains surrounded the deep dark waters of the lake where he rowed his boat. She was called *The Wanderer*.

A trout splashed up with a lively tail flip, and Jo rested on his oars and decided to bait a hook and try his luck. From shore the smoke of a campfire drifted toward him, and he imagined the meal he would have when he caught his fish. Probably he'd have a swim before supper.

The harsh noise of a buzzer brought him back

to the chair in the hotel room, and he got up and answered the door. It was a waiter with the chicken sandwich and the ice cream his mother had ordered for him.

"Kind of lonesome all by yourself, isn't it, sonny?" asked the waiter kindly.

Jo stiffened. "No," he answered briefly.

The waiter gave him a smile Jo didn't like and went out closing the door.

*The Wanderer's* spell was broken. Jo flipped the pages of the book and came to one that said *My Horse.* He took a bite from the sandwich and stared at the picture. Saddled, bridled, waiting to be mounted and ridden away stood a horse. Her kind inquiring face turned toward Jo for the lump of sugar he always gave her before he sprang into the saddle.

Where would they go this time? Up Lookout Mountain, he decided, as he flipped a page and took another bite of sandwich. The ice cream was melting into a dark pool, but Jo, unhurried, was far away. The sweating horse climbed willingly up the steep trail through the pine trees.

The saddle leather creaked. The sun beat down. Jo could smell the pungent carpet of pine needles. He took a pull of water from a canteen slung on the saddle and decided to turn off the trail and find a stream so his horse could drink too.

When the buzzer of the door sounded suddenly, he couldn't think for a moment what it was.

A bellhop in tight jacket and trousers, his pillbox hat aslant, stood holding a tray with a telegram on it.

Jo reached for the yellow envelope.

"Maybe I shouldn't leave it with you," said the bellhop. "It's for Mrs. Davis."

"I'll give it to her, she's my mother," said Jo. "She'll be back by and by."

"Well, sign here," said the bellhop, offering a pencil.

Jo scribbled his name on the slip and the bellhop left. His cocky hat and tight waist made him look like a walking tin soldier as he disappeared down the hall.

Jo laid the telegram on the table and went back to looking at the book. There were extra blank pages in it because when he found something really nice in a magazine he would add it to his collection of places to go. But for once the book's magic didn't work; it couldn't take him out of the hotel room. Jo knew what was holding him there—the thin yellow telegram was a weightless anchor that wouldn't let him go. What was inside that envelope? Did it tell that his father was dead? Or did his father want him back? Maybe he missed Jo and his mother. "I realize we never had any fun together. Let's all try again and be different this time." Maybe that's what the telegram said.

Only once had Jo's father been really cross with him. Usually he just didn't want to be bothered to notice that he had a boy. The time he was really cross he scared Jo. "You are a bad boy and I could send you to a reform school for this," he had said. What Jo had done was to take a stone and scratch the words "don't go" on the door of his father's beautiful new car. He had suddenly felt, while his parents were dressing to go out, that he just couldn't bear to be left all alone again in the house, the silent frightening house.

When they had finally left, all angry and distant, he had never felt so lonely and lost before, so guilty, so bad, so unworthy of love. He had remembered a movie he had once seen about a boy who was a burglar and who was sent away to a reform school. The movie had made a great impression on Jo. It hadn't shown the boy actually in the reform school. It had ended with his being led away by a couple of policemen, and Jo had felt cheated. "What goes on in a place like that?" he wondered. Do they beat you up or what do they do? In his heart he knew his father would never send him to such a place. Anyway, you don't get dragged off by a couple of policemen just for scratching your family's car. But his father had been mad, really sore, and Jo had suddenly remembered about a boy a couple of classes ahead of him whose family had sent him off to a strict military academy "to

8

get some discipline," because he had broken a lot of windows on purpose.

You never knew; you could be sent away.

He was roused from his thoughts by the sound of a key in the lock. The door opened and his mother came gaily into the room.

"I brought you some big fat salted nuts from the party," she said, smiling. "The kind you like, cashews," and she started to open her purse.

But just then she saw the telegram and, leaning over, she picked it up, tore the flap open and read the message.

Her face became grave. "Come here, Joey," she said, using the name she had called him by when he was little. "Sit down beside me on the sofa. There's something I want to tell you."

Jo did as he was told, eying his mother anxiously. He began to feel uneasy and afraid.

As if she were imploring him to understand, Jo's mother put her hand on his knee and began all in a rush. "I'm going to get married. You don't know him but you'll like him, Jo. I was going to have you meet him and then suddenly he had to go away. He's in Hawaii on business and we're going to be married there. We'll come and get you as soon as we come home."

"Where will I stay?" asked Jo, his voice only a whisper and his blue eyes, fixed on his mother's face, darkened with hurt.

She squeezed his hand. "That's what the telegram's about. It's from your grandmother and grandfather, asking you to stay with them in Freetown, New York. You've never met my mother and father—which is awful, really. I suppose your father and I were very selfish, but we never went East for a vacation and we never invited them here. Yes, it was selfish," she repeated, "but maybe I didn't want them to see that your father and I weren't happy together."

Jo didn't speak, he just kept on looking at his mother.

"They want you to come and stay with them," she repeated. "Honestly they do. And you'll like them—you remember you've always liked the Christmas presents they've sent you."

"Why can't I stay with Dad?" Jo asked tensely.

"I wish you could," his mother answered. "But he's going to be traveling on business most of the summer, and it just wouldn't work."

"Oh," said Jo dully.

"Honestly, you'll like your grandparents," his mother said again.

"Can't I stay with you?" asked Jo.

"I can't take you to Hawaii, Joey dear," his mother answered, "but we'll come and get you later."

Jo didn't say anything, but thought to himself, "I wonder if she means it."

# 2

It was the fifteenth of May, and Flight 202 was about to take off from the Cincinnati airport. The giant silver bird was about to carry Jo off like an insect in its stomach. At least that is the way Jo felt when he boarded the plane and the door slammed shut and the engines began to rev up. He had never flown before and a little feeling of trapped panic fluttered through him.

From his seat by a window he peered around

a fat man sitting next to him. A sailor across the aisle was yawning and opening a magazine. The pretty woman next to the sailor was putting on lipstick. The sailor said something that made her laugh, and Jo relaxed a bit when he saw that they were enjoying themselves.

Where was the seat belt he was supposed to fasten? The man next to him (who took up so much room he seemed to bulge into Jo) fumbled about and finally managed to dredge up two lengths of belt which he fastened over his stomach. Then he settled back, closed his eyes and seemed to fall asleep.

Jo began to fumble for his own belt, at the same time trying not to stick his elbow into the fat man. A pretty girl with kind laughing eyes and a cheerful smile walked toward him down the aisle. She wore a blue uniform and Jo guessed she must be the stewardess. Without any fuss, she leaned across the dozing man and fastened Jo's belt for him. "Leave it on until the sign flashes off. O.K.?" she said, smiling.

Jo nodded. "O.K.," he agreed. The girl made

him feel lots better. If a girl could enjoy flying day after day he knew he was going to enjoy it too.

The plane moved slowly down the runway, stopped, and turned ponderously around. The sound of the engines grew louder; the plane vibrated slightly. Out the window he could see a blur of giant propellers turning.

Then with a shaking roar the plane moved forward, faster—faster! Jo was one tight knot of waiting-to-see-what-next when suddenly he experienced a lovely peaceful feeling as he saw the ground fall away below him. The plane was air-borne and steadily rising.

He looked about him. The fat man was still sleeping and had begun to snore. The couple across the aisle were laughing over a picture they had found in the magazine.

The pretty stewardess stopped beside Jo's seat with an armful of magazines. "Which one do you want, *Look, Life, The Saturday Evening Post?*" She held them toward him and he chose one. He began to feel like a king. This was the life all right. He thought he would be a pilot when he finished school.

His mother had bought him a new gray suit for his trip, and he was wearing a red tie with white stripes. His shoes were new, too. He turned the pages of one of the magazines. But mostly he looked out the window. Below him was a giant map of streams, lakes, fields and forests. Suddenly, the plane's big silver wing was all he could see and the rest was misty white. "Why,"

thought Jo, "this is what it is like to be inside a cloud! This is great! What a life—I'd like to keep flying forever!"

The fat man gave a snort like a buffalo, woke up, and looked at his watch. That made Jo remember that before long the plane was going to land and he would meet his grandparents and sleep in a place he had never seen before. "I'm the boy nobody wants," he thought.

A cold feeling came into his fingers and his mouth began to be dry. What would his grandfather and his grandmother look like? Would his grandfather have a long white beard, and his grandmother be all bent over and leaning on a stick. Jo was rather good at arithmetic and he began to figure how old they might be. His mother had married when she was eighteen and Jo knew she was now thirty-one. If his grandmother and his grandfather had married when they were about twenty, you could add thirty-one to twenty and you got fifty-one. How old acting were people who were about half a hundred years old?

16

Jo bit his nails and looked out the window. It would be nice to be a pilot and then he wouldn't have to live with anybody. Probably pilots had bunkhouses where they played cards and read comics. He decided he'd be a pilot, and then it wouldn't matter that his mother didn't want him and he wouldn't have to live with any old grandparents either.

"Aw, what do I care," said Jo to himself. "People. Who cares about people? I'm going to be a pilot and fly way up high above all those people down there. They don't make any difference." He pulled a handkerchief out of his gray suit pocket and blew his nose hard.

The fat man turned toward him. "Hay fever?" he asked.

"Ugh, well, sort of," said Jo.

"Dust," said the man. "It's dust that does it." He closed his eyes and almost at once began to snore.

The stewardess walked down the aisle passing out lemonade.

"Thanks," said Jo, and drank thirstily.

A few minutes later she came back and collected the cups. "Taste good?" she asked.

"Yes, it sure did," said Jo.

The plane droned on through the skies and Jo kept his face to the window and imagined he was the pilot following a course.

After a time Jo noticed that the sign had blinked on again: *No Smoking—Fasten Your Seat Belts.* Down the aisle came the stewardess smiling and glancing right and left to check that the orders were being obeyed.

Presently Jo felt a sinking, jolting movement and glanced about him in alarm to see how others were taking it. He was afraid the plane was falling, yet everyone else looked relaxed and calm. Gazing out the window Jo noticed a runway ahead. So they were landing! He was about to meet his grandparents.

Lower, lower sank the big plane. Closer and closer the ground appeared. Jo felt a little sick and didn't look out the window any more. Suddenly, with a startling bump, the plane's wheels made contact with ground, the engines roared, then quieted as they taxied up the runway. "Please remain seated until the plane comes to a full stop," said the stewardess, who herself was walking about.

All at once the engines were silent, the plane was still. People unfastened their seat belts and began collecting their coats and parcels.

Jo looked out the plane window and saw a small crowd waiting by a gate. Someone would be there to meet him—he hoped.

Following his seatmate down the ramp, he half stumbled as he looked at the waiting people. There was no man with a long gray beard. He didn't see an old woman leaning on a stick. When passengers ahead of him reached the gate, relatives stepped forward with cries of joyful recognition, babies were kissed, parcels exchanged hands.

Jo continued through the gate feeling thoroughly bewildered and very lost. Suddenly, a man with a springy step walked toward Jo. The man's hair was sandy brown and rumpled, and he had blue eyes like Jo's. The neck of his shirt

19

was open and the legs of his blue jeans were stuffed into rough boots.

"Hi!" said the man, and smiled.

"Hi!" said Jo, and smiled a little.

"We'll find your bag," said the man, and led the way toward the airport terminal. "Where's your baggage check?"

Jo fished about in his pockets and produced it. While they waited for the baggage, the man hummed a little tune beneath his breath and looked around with interest. He didn't look at Jo any more, but Jo had a feeling that the man was pleased with him. They stood there together quite relaxed. Suddenly Jo wondered, "Maybe this man isn't my grandfather at all—perhaps he's someone sent to get me. He doesn't look like a grandfather, he looks too young." So he asked, "Are you my grandfather?"

The man looked at him and his blue eyes twinkled in his tanned face. "Of *course* I'm your grandfather, Jo," he said. "Didn't you know it at once? I knew the minute I saw you that you were my grandson," and he gave a couple of

20

gay shuffling steps with his big boots as if he wanted to get started on his way.

Just then Jo's bag was handed out. His grandfather let him carry it, which made Jo realize that he wasn't considered any weakling but was supposed to do a man's work.

"Don't call me Grandfather, call me Gramp," Jo was instructed as they left the terminal and walked toward an old station wagon parked at a meter.

Gramp opened up the back end, and reaching for Jo's bag, tossed it inside where it lay among a saddle, two bridles, and a violin. "Just open the front door and get in," he said, "the dog doesn't bite."

Jo did as he was told and saw a face with floppy ears looking at him. A long tail began to wag a brown and white body back and forth, and a pink tongue licked Jo's face in such an enthusiastic welcome that he just had to gather the dog into his arms so he could struggle into the car.

"What kind of dog is he?" asked Jo.

"A sort of a beagle," said Gramp. "His name is Ridiculous."

"Oh," said Jo, stroking the dog's head and fondling his long cool ears. "What is it?"

"No," said Gramp, "his name *is* Ridiculous, Rid for short."

The dog, satisfied that he had thoroughly welcomed Jo, put his head on the boy's lap and went to sleep.

Gramp started the car and off they drove in the direction of Freetown.

"Do you believe dogs should sleep in kennels or in the house?" asked Gramp.

Jo was surprised. No one was in the habit of asking his opinion. His parents' friends had sometimes tried to make conversation with him, asking him how old he was, whether he liked school, or remarking that he had grown. But here was an adult asking him a serious question and expecting an answer.

"In the house," said Jo with conviction.

"Good!" said Gramp, "that's what I think, too. Maybe it would be a good idea if Rid slept in your room."

22

Jo stroked the dog's head. "Would you like to, Rid?" he asked. The dog thumped his tail on the seat.

"That's the answer," said Gramp with satisfaction. "He would like to."

They drove along in silence past farms where, in the late afternoon light, the barns cast long shadows. Grass was lush and green in the fields and the trees looked as if they had shaken freshly washed leaves onto their branches.

"Why do you think cows lie down just before it's going to rain?" asked Gramp eagerly.

Jo didn't know they did and said so.

"Well, it's an old belief that I am checking on," said Gramp. "You check too," he advised.

"Three more miles," announced Gramp after quite a long silence. Jo noticed his grandfather never talked to make conversation. If there was something he wanted to say he said it with emphasis and enjoyment. The rest of the time Jo found that riding along beside him was quiet and comfortable.

"I like the spring," said Jo, "but I've never been out in the country in spring before."

"Spring is nice," said Gramp as they rattled past an orchard full of apple blossoms.

"Do you play the violin?" asked Jo, remembering the one he had seen in the back of the car.

"Yes," answered Gramp, "and your grandmother plays the piano. Why don't you learn to play the flute?" he asked with sudden inspiration. "There are some nice pieces of music written for violin, piano, and flute."

"Um, maybe," answered Jo doubtfully.

"Why don't you take off your coat and tie and be comfortable?" inquired Gramp, running his hand through his hair so it stood on end. "I always believe in being comfortable," he added emphatically.

"I think I would wake up Rid," Jo replied with a worried frown.

Gramp laughed. "Oh he'd go back to sleep again. You can't keep him awake in a car."

As Jo struggled out of his coat, his head turned toward the window just as a big sign marking a driveway with a closed iron gate came into view. He couldn't miss what the sign said: *Black Hill Reform School*. He craned his neck trying to catch a glimpse of the building or one of the inmates. He didn't see a soul, not even a keeper. Probably the boys were all shut up behind bars. He wanted to ask Gramp about the school but his tongue was stilled by the picture in his mind's eye—the picture of his father standing beside the scratched car, his face livid with anger. Jo seemed to hear that voice saying, "I could send you to reform school for this!" The memory paralyzed Jo and made him unable to ask a simple question.

Gramp gave a sidelong look at his grandson and apparently decided it was hunger that made the freckles stand out on the pale face, for he stepped hard on the accelerator. "I know what I hope there is for supper," he said, smacking his lips. "I hope there's steak with onions and apple pie with cheese."

Jo said nothing. He stroked the dog's head which had dropped back into its place on his knee. With his other hand he slowly worked his tie loose and pulled it off.

"Buttoned shirts always feel too tight," observed Gramp.

Jo fumbled and undid his collar.

The cool May breeze coming through the car window touched his neck and it felt good. The dog's head was warm on his lap. Unpleasant thoughts began to fade into the background, and he looked with interest at a farmhouse they were passing. He saw a cat on the front porch eating its supper out of a dish. Near the barn a man was leading a calf that didn't want to walk.

The car's engine coughed when Gramp changed into second gear to negotiate a rather steep hill. "Freetown's just around the next curve —hope you won't be disappointed," he remarked. "It's a pretty small place. No movie."

"What do people do?" wondered Jo. Probably they all had television.

As the car rounded the curve a cluster of houses and stores came in sight. "Here's the big city," said Gramp. They passed a garage with an old and battered car standing out in front. Next to the garage was the Busy Bee Diner and then a store that looked as if it sold hardware.

Jo noticed a grocery store with a street running off beside it on which there seemed to be houses needing paint. "Which of these would be

Gramp's?" he wondered. But the car lurched on past the street and didn't turn.

He had now begun to look tensely about him to discover the home where he was going to live —maybe forever. His heart sank. They passed the drugstore and he saw another street with houses; poorer-looking than the others he had noticed. But the car rattled out of the village, with Gramp waving to some people standing on a corner.

"Our house is on a hill—think you'll like the view," said Gramp.

Jo hoped the car would hold up until they got there. He began to feel a little tired because it was past supper time. The sun, almost down now, was a big gold ball that touched the horizon.

They had left the village well behind them and were skirting a wood of pine and nut trees when Gramp put on the brakes and swung suddenly to the left between two large stone gateposts. A single-lane drive wound ahead of them through woods where the last golden light of the sun filtered through the fresh green leaves. A thousand birds sang good-night songs. Rid scrambled to his feet, slipping and clawing on Jo's lap, and pushed his head out the window—he began to smell the smell of home.

Suddenly the rattling car came out into the open. Ahead of them, a very large house shaded by huge trees stood in the middle of a great lawn. It took Jo a moment to realize that it *was* a house for it was so covered and smothered in vines that it looked more like a green hill.

Sheep grazed on the lawn. "How do you like our wooly lawn mowers?" Gramp inquired. "Never have to cut the grass. They do it for me." He pulled off to the side of the drive. "Have to say good night to the girls," he explained, and he reached for a paper bag in the back of the station wagon as Rid tumbled out and disappeared into the woods. "Take a few carrots and make friends," Gramp suggested, opening the bag.

They stood beside a post-and-rail fence which bordered the drive and Gramp whistled. At first Jo saw nothing. Evening was coming on and the light was soft and beginning to be dim, and frog noises were taking the place of bird voices. He smelled an overpowering scent of lilacs and noticed a huge hedge of purple blossoms on the other side of the drive. The sweetness and peace of the evening lay all about. Presently Jo saw horses walking quietly toward them switching their tails.

"Here come the mares," said Gramp with satisfaction. "Nice bunch, aren't they?"

Close at the mares' sides tiny foals with baby faces and curly tails trotted on stilt-like legs. They looked like toys.

"There you are!" cried Gramp with a joyful note in his voice, and he slid between the split rails of the fence.

"Break the carrots in half and offer a piece on the flat of your hand," said Gramp casually. "The babies, of course, don't eat them—they drink their mother's milk." He wandered about in the midst of the herd, patting and feeding and complimenting the mothers on the beauty of their offsprings.

Jo was still on the outside of the fence. He broke a carrot, and holding it on the flat palm of his hand as he saw Gramp do, offered it over the top of the rail. A brown mare strolled toward him, neck outstretched, ears pricked, blowing slightly through her nose. Jo stood fast, still offering the carrot, and he felt the horse's soft lips tickling his palm as the carrot was gently removed. Then he heard the sharp crunch of raw carrot being chewed while the mare looked at him expectantly to see whether he had more.

Cautiously he slid under the fence, and standing beside the mare, offered her the other piece. Gramp was nearby, his arm flung over a mare's neck. He leaned there comfortably while he ruffled the mane of her little foal which crowded close.

Suddenly Jo felt himself bumped in the rear. A tiny baby horse was pushing close to him. He put out his hand too quickly, and the foal bounded away and ran close to the mare Jo had been feeding. Putting its little head low and then up under its mother's belly, it began to drink

30

milk with little pulling jerks of its head. All the time its curly tail whisked back and forth in glee at the good warm taste.

Jo gave the mother another piece of carrot.

"Grass and carrots make good milk for the babies," said Gramp with satisfaction. "I'm hungry myself, aren't you?" he asked suddenly.

Jo said he was. He ran his hand through his hair and it stood on end. He could smell the good smell of horse on his hand. All at once he was *very* hungry.

"Where has Rid disappeared to?" said Jo, looking about anxiously.

"Oh he's hunting a rabbit, I expect," laughed Gramp. "He'll be right back to get his supper. Get in the car, Jo," he said as he settled himself behind the wheel. They clanked up the drive to the front of the house. When the motor quieted Jo could hear someone playing a rippling, crashing tune on a piano.

"Chopin's *Polonaise*," said Gramp, whistling along with the piano as he pulled out Jo's bag.

As they came through the door into an immense cool hall smelling of purple and white lilacs, the music stopped. A woman appeared, stepping lightly, her hands outstretched in greeting. Her silver hair was tied back with a blue ribbon and her skirt floated around her as she walked.

"Welcome to Strawberry Hill, Jo!" she said, kissing him warmly on the cheek.

He was glad she didn't talk about his mother just then because he didn't know *how* to talk about her. He loved his mother, but she didn't want him. Even right now, as he thought about her, he wanted to strike out at something and hurt it. He looked shyly at his grandmother and saw that she looked like his mother. But now that he was close to his grandmother's face he could see clusters of little lines here and there. All the lines around her mouth and eyes got deeper when she laughed; he guessed they had been made by laughing.

"Come on, Jo, wash up!" she cried gaily. To his surprise she appeared glad to have him there.

# 3

"What's for supper, what's for supper?" asked Gramp as he led the way into the big dining room where a fire burned cheerfully in a fireplace adding light to the room which was lit by candles. Paintings hung on the walls. One was of a man on a horse and two were landscapes in heavy frames.

Gramp pulled out a chair for Jo's grandmother and seated her at the long table set for three.

"Sit here, Jo," she said, indicating the chair on her right.

"Beefsteak and onions as I live and breathe!" cried Gramp. "Just what I hoped for."

A very fat young woman with yellow hair done in braids around her head waddled in and out with platters. "Excellent, Freedle, excellent!" cried Gramp as he buttered a hot biscuit and then spread it liberally with comb honey.

"What did you say her name was?" asked Jo when the plump young woman had returned to the kitchen.

"Freedle," said Gramp, "Freedle Popinpoose."

Jo looked as if he didn't believe it.

"Yes," said his grandmother quickly and quietly as Freedle reappeared carrying an apple pie and a plate of cheese, which she set on the sideboard. "Yes, it's Freedle Popinpoose."

Suddenly there was a clatter of claws on the old polished floor as Rid skidded around the corner and came panting and wagging up to the table.

"Are you supposed to feed him in the dining room?" asked Jo, eying the few scraps of steak gristle and fat left on his otherwise empty plate.

"No, of course not," said Gramp sternly. "But I do," he laughed gaily. "I do." And he dropped a piece of meat into Rid's open mouth. Jo looked sideways at his grandmother but she sat serenely smiling, apparently absorbed in her private enjoyment of a silver bowl of spring flowers in the middle of the table. Jo quickly popped a bit of fat into the dog's mouth.

Freedle cleared the last of the plates and said enticingly, "Ridiculous, I have a nice bowl in the kitchen. Come see." The dog skidded out of the dining room and through into the kitchen, his tongue drooling with anticipation.

"He understands English!" exclaimed Jo.

"Of course," said Gramp matter of factly. "All the animals on this place understand English. We speak English, don't we?"

Jo began feeling quite mixed up but happier and happier. His grandparents lived in a big house full of polished furniture with silver on the table and the walls hung with paintings. Yet Gramp paid no attention to clothes and drove a dreadful old car. All the values Jo had known were reversed. The grownups he knew had big new cars, expensive clothes just right for each occasion, and lived in small houses. The main feature of their living rooms nearly always was a television set. Tonight, on his way to the dining room, Jo had passed the living room with its huge fireplace and comfortable furniture and he hadn't been able to see a television set. There was, however, a piano with chairs and music stands grouped around. Apparently they made their own music.

"Gramp, are you rich?" asked Jo.

His grandfather looked a little startled. "Well now, what do you mean by rich? I'm rich in happiness."

"I mean money—do you have lots of money?"

"That is not supposed to be a polite question," said Gramp reprovingly. "But," said he, considering, "I feel a straight question deserves a straight answer. Yes," he said, "I have quite a lot of

money but I don't regard it as important. If I
have enough to eat, a roof over my head when
it's cold, people and animals I'm fond of, and a
lot of good country to move around in, whatever amount of money I have in the bank is certainly secondary. No, not secondary," he said
after a pause, "fifthly." Then after another
pause, during which he was obviously thinking,
"No, hundredthly. There are *so* many things that
matter more," he declared, with finality. "Like
stars," he said suddenly. "Come on, let's look at
the stars," and he jumped up from the table,
strode around to his wife's chair and pulled her
gaily to her feet. "Now that we've finished the
pie, let's have a look at 'the spacious firmament
on high!'" cried Gramp enthusiastically as he
led her by the hand to the door.

"Jo, your grandfather loves to quote," said his
grandmother laughing, and she held out a hand
to Jo so they left the dining room as a threesome.

The soft spring evening enfolded them as they
stepped out through glass doors that opened
from the dining room onto the terrace. Pale stars

showed in the sky and the moon was riding a little mound of clouds. The baaing of a sheep was the only sound.

"Now I wonder," exclaimed Gramp with excitement, "which of these stars we are looking at has life on it? Thousands, maybe millions, undoubtedly do, but which ones? Do you suppose the people up there are going to sleep or getting up? I wonder whether they are looking at our earth and speculating about possible life on it? Very interesting, very interesting," said Gramp, who stood with his head thrown back and his mouth slightly open as he regarded the starry sky. His arm slipped around his wife's waist as they enjoyed the night together. Jo liked that because he felt they weren't going to fight the way his parents always had.

But what a funny sort of grandfather! He is so terribly interested in everything, thought Jo. He never acts bored like most grownups do. Yes, to Jo he seemed remarkably young, younger even than his grandmother who gave the feeling of being young herself, perhaps because her silvery hair was tied with a blue ribbon, perhaps because she walked as gaily as a girl.

Jo began to catch his grandparents' conviction that there weren't enough hours in the day or night to see and do all the wonderful things the world offered. It was as if he had been living in a dark hole and had suddenly come up into sunlight.

Freedle Popinpoose appeared in the doorway, her yellow braids shining in the light behind her.

"If I may say so, Mrs. Shaw, the boy needs his sleep. Shall I show him his room?" she asked.

"You probably would like to unpack and settle your things," said his grandmother turning toward Jo. "A box of clothes your mother sent on by express arrived yesterday and it's in your room. Breakfast is at eight and you will hear a gong at seven-thirty to wake you up. Sleep well."

She looked as if she expected him to kiss her good night and he stepped forward hesitantly.

"Good night—" He paused.

"Gran," said his grandmother quickly, and she took a step forward and kissed him on the forehead, at the same time giving his shoulder a little squeeze.

"Good night, Gran; good night, Gramp," said Jo.

"See you in the morning," called Gramp.

Jo followed Freedle into the house and through the dining room to the cool, lilac-scented hall. A big bronze gong like a temple bell hung on a heavy wooden pedestal near the stairs. A cloth-covered mallet hanging nearby gave Jo an almost irresistible impulse to give the gong a bong.

"Is that what wakes us up in the morning?" he asked Freedle.

"Ya, I hit it five times at seven-thirty each morning. Your grandpa don't like alarm clocks. This he likes."

"Can I hit it sometimes?" asked Jo.

Freedle shook her head. "I do it just like your grandpa likes," she said with finality. "Come, I show you your room," and she planted a flat foot on the first step of the staircase.

"I'm the one who has to think all the practical thoughts around here," grumbled Freedle as she puffed ahead of him like a slow-moving engine. "Your grandma is only interested in writing poetry and taking care of her rose garden, and your grandpa thinks all the time about horses. The rest of the time they play music."

Carrying his suitcase, Jo climbed very slowly behind Freedle. He had a question he very much wanted to put to someone and he felt it would be easier to ask Freedle than either of his grandparents. Trying to make his voice casual, and feeling glad that he was addressing Freedle's back, he began: "There was a funny old sign I noticed coming along this afternoon. It was just some sort of funny old sign—not that I care," he added hastily, "but I just sort of wondered about it."

"What sign?" asked Freedle as she thumped and puffed up the stairs ahead of him.

"Black Hill Reform School," said Jo, almost choking over the words. "Not that I care, you know, I just sort of wondered what sort of a place it is."

Freedle's fat shoulders in front of him shook indignantly. "Don't talk to me about them bad boys. Burglars, murderers. Sometimes I think I move away. Them bad boys is only one mile from here. Maybe they kill me in my bed."

They had reached the top of the stairs and Freedle paused a moment in the dark passageway. Far down at the end, a window, half obscured by the leafy vines that covered the house, let in a pale moonbeam. For some reason Freedle did not turn on the light but led the way down the spooky moonlit corridor.

"This way," she said. "You follow me."

Suddenly she paused in front of a closed door.

"In this room comes the ghost. . . ." She whispered and hesitated as if to listen.

Silence. Complete silence. Then, borne on the beam of moonlight, through the open window at the end of the passage, the peaceful baa of a sheep drifted to them. Vine leaves moving in the night breeze formed shadows like live things on the floor. Jo shivered and listened, but behind the mysterious closed door all was silence.

"What do you mean a *ghost?*" Jo had copied Freedle's cautious whisper as he asked the question. "Pooh, I don't believe in ghosts!" he said a little louder and looked behind him.

"No?" questioned Freedle. "Your grandpa does," she declared.

"What sort of things does the ghost do?" asked Jo, trying to make the words sound as if he felt they were of no importance.

Freedle had resumed her ponderous walk down the corridor and her voice floated back to him over her shoulder.

"There's a smell of violets sometimes in the room and a window that was locked stands open," said Freedle somberly.

Near the end of the corridor she opened a door to the left and switched on the light. Jo saw a big high-ceilinged room which dwarfed a huge old-fashioned double bed standing against one wall. He next noticed a chest of drawers with a tall mirror surmounted by an eagle. The floor of the room was carpeted in dark red. A desk and a chair were in one corner and a few easy chairs and a table or two stood about. Book-shelves lined one of the walls and on the rest of the wall space hung old prints of race horses. There was a window seat in front of one of the heavily-curtained windows. In a strange kind of way the room gave Jo both a feeling of cheerful-ness and, perhaps because of its size, a shiver of spookiness.

He set his suitcase down on the floor. Freedle was about to leave him. He felt terribly alone but didn't want to ask where his grandparents slept.

"The bathroom you use is the door across the passage," said Freedle as she prepared to leave.

Desperately Jo cast about for something to say to keep her a moment longer.

"Are you an American?" he blurted out.

"Well, no," said Freedle, placidly smoothing her coil of yellow braids. "Your grandma and grandpa picked me up in Europe." It sounded as if Freedle were a souvenir or a package of post-cards they had collected on one of their trips abroad, the way she said it.

"Have you been over long?" asked Jo, trying to carry on the conversation so as to delay her departure.

"Three years," declared Freedle. "I like it here."

"Why is this place called Strawberry Hill?" he inquired, still trying to keep the conversation alive.

"In June fields all around are full of wild strawberries. Very pretty but hard to pick," said Freedle. She started to waddle toward the door and Jo knew this time she was going to go.

Like a life raft the thought of Ridiculous drifted into his mind.

"Rid is supposed to sleep in my room!" he declared urgently.

"O.K.," said Freedle, "I'll send him to the stairs and you whistle."

Jo stood in his bedroom doorway and listened to Freedle's footsteps retreat down the corridor and then thump-thump down the stairs. He began to whistle short, piercing, quick whistles with his lips puckered extra tightly.

A skittering of claws and a galumpfing on the stairs echoed toward him. Suddenly Rid burst into view out of the darkness, tail wagging, long ears floating back as he streaked around the corner into the bedroom.

"Hi, Rid, good old boy!" cried Jo, and he bent down and patted the dog over and over while the skin was almost licked off his cheek in exchange. "Gosh I'm glad to see you, Rid!" declared Jo feelingly as he shut the door.

"Probably I should do a lot of unpacking," he thought. But he felt too sleepy. He fished his pajamas out of the suitcase and then ran to rescue the bottom part from Rid, who was dragging it across the room, head held high, tripping at each step over the trailing legs. Jo had to laugh.

"Bad boy!" he said with mock disapproval.

He dreaded crossing the gloomy corridor to brush his teeth and did it as fast as possible, taking Rid with him for company.

Back in the bedroom he snapped off the light. He jumped into the huge bed and snuggled under the covers. Ridiculous put his front paws on the edge and seemed to ask, "Where shall I sleep?"

"Come on, boy, come on, Rid!" cried Jo and patted the place beside himself. After a couple of false leaps, the dog made it and scrambled all over Jo whining excitedly, but soon settled down beside him.

Freedle had opened the window before she left, and Jo could hear a monotonous chorus of peeper frogs. He remembered how vines covered the house and he felt himself snug in a green cave as he listened to the night voices.

Without his dog he would have been lost in the enormous bed, but Rid was comforting, like the bear that he had always taken to bed with him when he was a little boy.

The leaves of the vine outside his window rustled softly in the evening breeze, and a sheep's baa was the last thing he heard before drifting off to sleep.

# 4

Bong, bong, bong, bong, bong. A booming gong penetrated Jo's slumbers. Where was he? A wiggling beside him made him remember Rid, then Gran and Gramp, then Freedle, and he opened his eyes to brilliant sunshine pouring in through the vine-hung window. The morning air was vibrant with bird songs.

One bound and he was out of bed and onto the window seat, where he leaned on the sill with Rid beside him and looked at the view spread out before his eyes. Beneath the window the sheep were grazing, and where the lawn ended at the back of the house, the land fell steeply away into woods. He could look far off across a mist-filled valley to distant hills beyond.

He pulled a pair of blue jeans and a shirt out of his suitcase and in doing so uncovered his book. Impatiently he stuffed it into a bureau drawer and pushed it far to the back. He was beginning to realize that there was too much to do in the real world to bother with a book of dreams.

He hastily tied his sneakers, for Rid was dancing around, ears flopping, tail wagging, and begging to be let out. As they raced each other down the corridor to the stairs Jo forgot even to glance at the door of the ghost room.

Breakfast was laid out on hot trays on the sideboard in the dining room, and after letting Rid outdoors, Jo rather hesitantly picked up a plate and wondered whether to serve himself.

Just then Gramp appeared in the doorway rubbing his hands with glee at the thought of a fine breakfast.

"Hope you slept well!" he commented cheerfully, and without waiting for an answer, waved Jo toward the platters of bacon and eggs, sausages and buttered toast.

"Do you know how to paint?" Gramp inquired as they companionably munched their toast and marmalade.

"Pictures, you mean?" asked Jo doubtfully.

"No, actually I didn't mean pictures. Do you paint pictures?"

"No," said Jo, shaking his head emphatically.

"What I meant," explained Gramp, mumbling a little through a bite of sausage, "was regular painting. There's a boat needs painting down at the pond. We might ride over on our horses and have a look at it."

"Ride!" Jo had never ridden except in his dream world where, of course, he was brilliant.

He choked a little over a bite of toast. Gramp took no notice but rose and went out the glass doors.

"I'll meet you in half an hour out in front where the mares are. You can bring Rid," he added. "He enjoys going along with the horses."

A light, quick step sounded in the hall.

"Good morning, Gran," said Jo, rising as his grandmother entered the dining room.

She looked so much like his mother it startled him, but the way she came into the room was different. It had always seemed that his mother was making a stage entrance; she seemed to be saying, "Here I am! How do you like my new dress?" With Gran it was different. As she came toward Jo her eyes were saying, "There you are. I'm glad to see you." She wasn't thinking about herself at all.

She kissed Jo warmly. She smelled of some nice kind of soap or something. He drew away from her a little—the hurt that was in him from his mother made him afraid to love her.

Even though she must have sensed his withdrawal, she smiled at him and asked, "Did I hear your grandfather say you were riding the horses to the pond today? I'll have some sandwiches put in your saddlebags." She rang a tinkly bell which was answered almost at once by the appearance of Freedle.

"Good morning, Freedle," Gran greeted her. "Two saddlebag lunches, please."

"Fish or meat?" asked Freedle.

Gran turned to Jo.

"Which do you like?" she asked smiling.

"Meat," answered Jo, without hesitation.

"It will have to be chicken, Mrs. Shaw," said Freedle. "They ate all the beef last night."

"That will be fine," answered Gran, and she picked up a plate and helped herself to an egg.

Freedle nodded and disappeared into the kitchen.

"She walks slowly," said Gran, "but she's a quick sandwich maker. Your lunches will be ready in a few minutes. Every day," she explained, "sandwiches are put out on the dining-room sideboard with little cartons of milk. In that way we can all be independent and take our lunches wherever we want. If you ask Freedle at breakfast time to make your sandwiches earlier because you want to go an an expedition, she'll get them ready for you."

This seemed like a wonderful idea to Jo. There

was a freedom about Strawberry Hill that made him feel rather dazed after the restricted life of suburbs and hotels, where his mother was always nagging him to do this or not to do that. Like a horse that has been kept in a stall and is suddenly let out into pasture, he was stunned by so much liberty.

"Where is the boat we are going to look at?" he asked.

"About three miles from here, on Ghostly Pond," his grandmother replied as she poured herself a cup of coffee.

"What a funny name! Is it your pond?" asked Jo.

"Oh yes, it's on the place," answered Gran, carefully dropping two lumps of sugar into her steaming coffee and stirring them slowly round. "Your grandfather named the pond. Some nights mist rises from the water in white, weaving vapors and your grandfather thinks it looks like ghosts. He adores the idea of ghosts," said Gran, laughing.

"If you thought it was a real ghost, wouldn't you be scared?" asked Jo.

"Perhaps," admitted Gran. "In this house—"
She paused as if undecided whether to go on.

Just at that moment, Freedle lumbered in with
two leather saddlebags stuffed with sandwiches.
She handed them to Jo. Out loud he thanked her,
but inside he was thinking, "She looks like a
human elephant. I wonder how much she eats."

Jo noticed that Gran seemed to have forgotten
what she had been going to say before Freedle
came in, so he murmured a good-by and, whistling for Rid, left the house. Followed by the
dog, he walked down the drive toward the field
where the mares were turned out. As he walked
he bit his nails.

Truth to tell, he felt a bit nervous and wondered whether his grandfather realized he had
never ridden before. He hoped he wouldn't make
a fool of himself.

Gramp was leaning on the pasture rail and
appraised Jo quizzically as he approached.

"Don't believe in riding in sneakers," he said.
"There are some jodhpur boots over in the stable
that I think will fit you. Ever ridden before?" he
asked.

"No," said Jo, and licked his dry lips.

"I want to introduce you to your horse. You'll like her," said Gramp enthusiastically.

"Where is she?" asked Jo. He could see the mares and foals off in the distance near a clump of trees.

"She's in a paddock next to the stable, and so is old Trumpet, the horse I'm going to ride," said Gramp, heading off down the drive. They passed the lilac hedge that Jo had smelled last night, and turned off behind it down a short lane to a green stable.

"We'll find those boots and get the tack ready before we bring in the horses." Gramp slid open the stable door and led the way into the tack room, where saddles and bridles were neatly arranged on pegs and racks. The room smelled of horse and well-oiled leather.

"This saddle looks about right for you, Jo." Gramp lifted a saddle from one of the racks and pulled a bridle from a peg.

"These aren't Western saddles, are they?" asked Jo, who had watched cowboys on television.

56

"No, they're English," his grandfather answered. "Each type of saddle has its purpose. Out West the cowboys need a saddle with a pommel or horn so they can hang their lariat on it. They also use it to hold cattle which have been roped for branding. Out on the plains and prairies there are no fences to jump, but here in the East there are—so we need saddles of a different sort. Those Western saddles aren't practical for Easterners. If you landed on one of those saddle horns after a four-foot jump it would be, let us say—uncomfortable?" He reached into a cupboard and pulled out a pair of boots.

"Try these for size," he suggested.

Jo kicked off his sneakers and slid into the short boots. They fitted him remarkably well.

"We'll leave your saddle and bridle on this bench for the moment. Come on," directed Gramp, "our horses are back here—I turned them out for a little grazing." He led the way from the tack room. They walked along the clean-swept concrete floor of the stable, between some empty box stalls well-bedded with deep straw that smelled fresh and good. The rear door slid open easily and Jo saw a paddock fenced with white boards. At the sound of voices and the noise of the sliding door the two horses lifted their heads.

"That gray is one of the gentlest horses I've ever owned. She was bred and raised on the place and has always been treated well. I trained her myself," said Gramp. "Notice her eye. She has a lovely, kind, dark eye, no white showing. If you get on well with her, she's your horse. The bay is old Trumpet, a great jumper."

Gramp gave a low whistle. A medium-size, silver-gray mare with a black mane and tail pricked up her ears and began to stroll toward them. Gramp opened the gate.

"Come along, Quicksilver!" called Gramp softly. "Come along, girl—we're going for a ride."

The horse approached at a leisurely smooth walk, stopping once or twice to lower her head and have a last bite of grass. Trumpet followed close behind.

"Come on, my beauty; come on, my girl," called Gramp, and he whistled again.

"Learn this whistle," he advised Jo, "and always give her a carrot or a few oats. Then she'll come when you want her. Here, you give her this carrot," and he pulled one from his pocket and handed it to Jo. "I'll give one to Trumpet. Here you are, Trumpet, good old boy.

"Just take your horse by the halter on the near

side—that's the left—and lead her into the stable. We'll clean them off and saddle up in there."

Jo reached out and put a hand on the gray's halter. He felt doubtful.

"Don't ever look at a horse when you're leading him or he won't follow," called Gramp.

Quietly and without fuss, Quicksilver walked beside Jo into the stable. With every step Jo felt more confident and pleased with himself and his horse.

"Snap that rope there onto her halter and she'll stand. I'll tie Trumpet up here," directed Gramp who followed leading the big bay horse.

"I'll give you a lesson in grooming. Here's a brush and currycomb. Watch me, Jo, and then do it yourself.

"That's right—that's all right, you've got the hang of it," Gramp smiled approvingly. "The horses are both pretty clean; we don't need to do much grooming today. Now comb out Quicksilver's mane and tail. Never walk behind a horse without letting him know you're going to do so.

60

People get kicked when horses are startled. Put your hand on her rump and let her know you're there. It's better to keep away entirely from a horse's heels, or else stay close so he can't get the room to kick you hard. There's not much punch to a fist one inch from your nose, but there's a lot an arm's length away. Same thing with a horse's legs."

Jo ran the comb through Quicksilver's black tail, then carefully and lovingly combed the fringe of glossy mane flat onto her neck. When he put his hand on her she felt warm and smooth and nice. He knew he was fumbling a lot but the mare took it all kindly and he began to love her.

"Now I'll show you how to bridle and saddle." Gramp picked up the gray's bridle from the bench where he had laid it. "I expect you to do this next time yourself. It's easy really," remarked Gramp cheerfully, as he slipped the bit into Quicksilver's willing mouth and adjusted the bridle over her ears. "See, nothing to it. Now get your saddle. That's right, put it right here."

Gramp pulled the saddle a little forward onto the horse's withers. "Fasten the girth yourself. Perfectly easy; you can fasten your own belt, can't you?" questioned Gramp impatiently as Jo hesitated. "Look, like this. That's right.

"Lead her outside and I'll show you how to mount."

Remembering not to look at the mare as he led her, Jo put his hand on the reins and his horse followed him, feet clop-clopping on the concrete then lightly thudding on the damp lane by the lilacs. Birds were singing. Jo's morning was full of light and happiness.

"Now pay attention to what I tell you," said Gramp, who had followed behind Jo and Quicksilver.

"Gather up your reins in your left hand, face the horse's rear, turn your left stirrup toward you, and put your foot in. Give a hop—come on, give a hop!"

Jo hopped and Gramp pushed his seat from behind. Rid, who had appeared from the other side of the hedge, helped by barking.

"Well, you're on," said Gramp with a grunt, "but that wasn't very good. Don't drop into the saddle with a bump, but let your knees take your weight before you lower your seat." Gramp patted the patient mare's glossy neck. "That's a good girl, Quicksilver. He'll do better next time.

"Now take your feet out of the stirrups and let's see about the length. Your ankle bones should just touch the bottom of the stirrups. Funnily enough these look about right. Stick your feet back in. Now look, this is the way you hold your reins. Never jerk a horse's mouth. This mare has a lovely mouth, so be sure you don't hang on by the reins. Just walk up and down the lane for a minute while I saddle Trumpet. Squeeze your legs together to make her move." Gramp gave the mare a last encouraging pat and disappeared into the stable, leaving Jo all alone high up on a horse.

Rid looked questioningly at him and wagged his tail then took a couple of ear-flopping leaps down the lane. "Let's go!" he seemed to say.

Jo squeezed his legs together and the mare

moved forward at a slow walk but started reaching with her head as Jo instinctively hung on too tight to the reins. Quickly he remembered what Gramp had said and slacked off.

It was a glorious feeling to be on a moving horse; Jo was thrilled and scared at the same time. He began to wonder how you turned around—steer like a bicycle, maybe. He pulled on the left rein and kept pulling, knowing he wasn't doing it just right; but the amiable mare took the hint and headed back toward the stable.

Gramp was just mounting and had seen the turn-around. He walked his horse down the lane toward Jo.

"Keep your hands closer together about an inch above the withers, don't pull your rein way out sideways like that—press with your legs as well as using your rein when you turn; that swings the horse's body around and not just his neck. You are doing all right though. Now turn her around to the right. Press with your legs again, keep the left rein steady, and pull slightly on the right rein. Good, that's better!"

Jo found himself riding beside Trumpet. They headed for a gate leading into a long field bordered by a wood. Every minute he felt better and more confident, but he hoped they would continue to go pretty slowly. Gramp had said Trumpet was a fine jumper. Was Quicksilver? Jo wondered whether he would ever learn to jump. The very thought thrilled him.

Gramp moved his big horse up beside the gate and, leaning over, unfastened the latch. The gate swung open enough to let the horses through and Jo watched, fascinated, as Trumpet (who was a trained gate horse) followed the gate back into place as Gramp pushed it and then allowed his rider to move him sideways with leg pressure until the gate was in place; then the old horse stood fast as Gramp redid the latch.

"Always close gates," he said. "Otherwise cattle or horses or sheep may get out and that is unforgivable." He patted Trumpet to praise him for a job well done.

Jo made a mental note. He had a feeling that Gramp was the sort of person who expected you to remember and did not intend to say things twice. *Close gates.* He'd remember.

A beautiful grassy field stretched out in front of them. The land had been grazed but clumps of weeds that didn't taste good to horses left tall patches. Rid found the trail of a rabbit and ran off joyfully, nose to ground, giving tongue in musical yaps.

"Let's trot a few steps," suggested Gramp. "Want to?"

Jo nodded.

Gramp pressed Trumpet into a slow, steady trot and Quicksilver kept beside him. Jo bumped along breathless and rather nervous but was careful not to jerk on the mare's mouth.

"Don't worry, the ground's nice and soft if you fall off," laughed Gramp. "Whoa!" he said, seeing Jo had had enough for the moment. "Try to post to the trot," he advised. "Grip with your knees and let the horse throw you up, then you won't bang down on her so hard. Did you notice her ears were back? It wasn't very comfortable for her."

They had reached a rail fence that bordered the wood.

"Someday soon we'll jump this." Gramp had dismounted and removed a couple of rails leaving a gap through which Jo urged his horse. Gramp led Trumpet through, and keeping the reins looped over his arm, he replaced the rails and remounted.

"Follow me into the woods. There's a nice path. We'll just walk. Keep your eyes open—lots of things to see. Leave a horse's length between us, and if Quicksliver gets too close hold her back but don't jerk."

The leaves of the trees sifted the sunshine which lay in spots and dapples on the ferns bordering the path. Birds sang and flew on short expeditions from tree to tree. A chipmunk passed like a flash over a fallen log, causing Jo's mare to prick up her ears and move her head sideways.

Gramp wore a small knapsack fastened over his shoulders with straps. Jo wondered what was in it. Gramp sat easily in the saddle, his body accommodating itself to the stride of the big bay horse. Jo tried to loosen up and not be so rigid, to sit more like Gramp.

"We're going to ford a stream," Gramp's voice floated back to Jo. "Give the mare her head and she'll pick her footing. Lean forward!" Trumpet began splashing his way slowly through the running water. Following behind, Quicksilver lowered her head to take a look at where she was going. Gramp was glancing back over his shoulder.

"That's right, give her her head. She'll take care of you."

It was a thrill hearing the splash of water all around him. Spray flew up and landed on his boots. He was really doing just what he had dreamed of in the book. As they came out onto the bank on the other side, Jo felt such gratitude to the mare for bringing him safely through that he patted her neck.

"Good Quicksie!" he whispered. After that it was the name he always called her by, his pet name, just for them.

Jo checked the leather bag of sandwiches fastened to his saddle, but it wasn't wet. Before him he could see bright sunlight; they were nearly out of the woods.

The path ended at a meadow which rose abruptly onto a steep hill where rocks showed through the scant soil.

"Gosh, that's steep. You don't suppose we're going up it?" wondered Jo, glancing apprehensively ahead of him.

Just then Rid rejoined them, soaking wet from swimming the stream, and shook himself in the sunshine.

Gramp called to Jo. "Hang onto her mane when we climb this hill; lean forward."

Jo drew a deep breath. He wanted to bite his nails but he didn't dare take his hands off the reins.

The horses, necks outstretched, taking strong, pulling strides with their forelegs and powerful thrusts with their hind legs, started up the steep incline.

"We don't have to go up here to get to the

pond but the view is wonderful from the top and I thought you'd enjoy it. I always do," Gramp added. He was leaning well forward on his horse's neck and Jo did the same.

Both horses were blowing a little as they came over the brow of the hill and pulled to a stop. Jo patted the mare's neck which was damp from the exertion of climbing. He felt gloriously exhilarated. He'd made it. It was fun.

They rested and looked off from their lofty position over the irregular checkerboard of plowed fields and grassy meadows. About a mile away Jo noticed a great pile of a building, forbidding as a fortress.

"What's that?" he asked, but he had guessed before his grandfather answered.

"That's Black Hill Reform School—we passed the gate, remember? I understand that sometime soon they're going to give the place up and build something more modern with a different name. High time!"

Jo said nothing, but again he wondered what the boys were like who lived in that gloomy place. What had they done to be sent there? What was it like behind those walls?

Gramp didn't seem to notice Jo's silence. "Well, Trumpet, are you rested?" he asked, and gave the big bay horse's neck an affectionate slap. "Let's move off. We'll go down the hill and skirt the wood—the pond's on the other side.

"Lean forward a little going down and take your weight off your horse's quarters. Look at that lazy dog waiting for us at the bottom of the hill!" laughed Gramp, and he pointed at Rid who sat smugly, saving his energy for rabbits.

To Jo the descent was even more of a thrill than the climb. With forelegs braced at every step and quarters shifting from side to side, the gray mare carefully made her way down the incline which, to Jo, seemed almost perpendicular.

He felt a certain amount of relief when they once more were on flat ground. Rid greeted them with tail wags and what Jo thought was an amused expression. He seemed to be saying, "Why go up there—no rabbits, you know."

"Try a little trotting," urged Gramp, "and see

71

whether you can do any better. That's right, up
—down—up—down. Now you've got it! See
how much better that feels, and Quicksilver's
ears are forward—she's more comfortable."

Quiet elation filled Jo because Gramp was
pleased with him.

The pond lay just beyond the north side of the
dense wood in a fringe of oak and white pine
trees. The clear water reflected blue sky. It
looked good enough to drink.

As if reading Jo's thoughts Gramp said, "Follow me along this path to the cabin, there's a
spring there. I wouldn't drink the pond water;
it's full of bacteria but it's all right for horses.
They like clear water, you know. A dog will
drink from a muddy puddle, but not a horse."

The cabin had been concealed by a clump of
pine trees which they rounded as they followed
the path. Built of logs with a low, thick chimney,
it was a real pioneer-type dwelling. A woodpile
was stacked against one wall, a bucket stood by
the front door, and at the back a spring trickled
over a black rock and ran off in a clear rivulet
into the pond.

"There's a corral over at the other side," said Gramp leading the way.

The horses picked up their feet in the under-brush and made their way over a few low, fallen trees.

"Sure-footed animals," remarked Gramp. "Wouldn't want them if they tripped over things. I like a horse that looks where he's going."

There was a wonderful woodsy smell of moss and rotting logs. Jo glanced down as Quicksie carefully looked for her footing. He saw a green fern with its tip curled like a question mark.

"Seldom come over to the pond," said Gramp, "never walk around. There's poison ivy here and I'm terribly allergic to it—much more so than most people. Look out for a vine that has three shiny leaves in a cluster."

Jo patted Quicksie's neck. She was such a clever horse; not one stumble over all this rough going.

"Here we are," said Gramp as they came into a sunny clearing where a little grass grew. He let down the bars of a small corral made of rough poles cut from the nearby woods. Two big oaks that had been left standing gave a little shade under which a horse could shelter from the summer sun.

"I'm leaving you for a couple of hours," Gramp remarked casually. "Unsaddle your horse and turn her loose in there. I've got to ride on to speak to a farmer whose place joins mine. He's putting up a new fence and I'd like him to put in a panel or two in the wire so we can jump it. Reasonable chap. We'll work it out together—never had any trouble with Tom Bruckel; he's a good neighbor."

Gramp unslung the knapsack from his back and held it out toward Jo who dismounted and took it from him.

"There's a can of paint and a brush in there —you can start on the boat. She's dry; she's pulled ashore down by that little dock." He jerked his head in the direction of the pond. Leaning in the saddle, Gramp felt the gray mare's neck with a practiced hand.

"We mostly walked today," he said. "Your horse is cool and dry so she can have water.

There's a bucket out in front of the cabin; just fill it in the pond and hang it on this hook inside the corral. I'll be back to help you saddle up. You've got your lunch?"

Jo nodded.

"I guess Rid would like to stay with you." Gramp looked down at the dog, who was standing close to Jo. "Always said to your grandmother, 'That dog would like to belong to a boy.' A year ago he was just a skinny puppy that wandered through the gate one day. Don't know where he came from. Always seemed to be looking for something, but now I guess he's found it," and Gramp smiled. "Well, see you in a couple of hours."

Jo stood watching as Trumpet and Gramp disappeared into the woods. Quite soon the faint snapping in the undergrowth ceased. He was alone except for his horse and his dog.

# 5

After he had unsaddled Quicksie, Jo hung the bridle on a post and laid the saddle on one of the bars of the corral. Then he took the bucket to the pond and brought it back brimful. He spilled a little climbing through the bars of the fence but there was a lot left. The mare lowered her muzzle to the cool water and sucked in great draughts. Then she raised her head, water slobbering from her lips, and with pricked ears looked off toward the woods where Trumpet had disappeared. She whinnied.

"Don't worry," said Jo, who was worried himself. "They'll come back." He stroked her soft neck and talked to her gently. By and by she quieted and lowered her head to crop the scant grass.

Whistling to Rid, Jo made his way around to the door of the cabin. The unoiled hinge creaked as he pushed his way in. A scuttle of some startled animal made him jump, and Rid raced to a tiny hole in the wall and whined. Jo looked around warily.

"Mice—or a chipmunk," he said to himself. "It's nothing." But his skin felt prickly.

The cabin must have been closed a long time for the earthen floor was damp and the place smelled musty.

"A good fire in the fireplace would help," thought Jo, "but I'm certainly not going to do anything about it today—I've got that boat to paint. Where's a cup, I wonder?—I'm thirsty."

In a rough cupboard standing in a corner of the single-room cabin he spied a few cups, plates, knives and forks. Two frying pans hung from nails on the wall. As he picked up one of the cups he saw a bunk against the wall. There was a rough brown blanket on it, but no pillow.

"Gosh, you could camp out here and fry your dinner in the fireplace!" he thought as he went around back to the spring.

The water tasted delicious; he drank two cupfuls and left the cup hanging on a twig.

As he undid the knapsack he wondered what color paint he would find. He looked at the label. "Red! Oh, that will look nice on the blue water."

With no difficulty he found the boat lying upside down in a bed of ferns. It was small and not heavy, and he tugged it into a more open spot and jacked it up on a couple of logs.

Behind him he heard Rid dragging something, and turned around. "Gosh, he's got the lunch bag! Drop it, you! Naughty boy!" But it was his own fault really—he'd unfastened the leather bag from his saddle and left it on the ground. "You're giving me the hint it's lunch time, aren't you, you rascal? You're pretty smart; you think you'll get some scraps." Jo leaned down and pulled the dog's long ears affectionately.

78

The sun was high in the sky so he figured it must be about twelve o'clock. In the excitement of exploring the cabin and finding the boat he hadn't realized how hungry he was. He sat down on a log and opened the saddlebag. Stuffed eggs, good; chicken sandwiches, wonderful; a raw carrot, ugh, but it was supposed to be good for your eyes, and if he was going to be a pilot . . . he'd eat a couple of bites and give the rest to Quicksie; a hunk of cheese, not bad; chocolate brownies with nuts, yum; and an apple. Freedle, he decided, had done well by him.

Jo started on an egg. Rid sat up on his hind legs and begged piteously, tongue hanging out and eyes pleading that he was starving to death. Before Jo began on a chicken sandwich he broke off a piece of the bread and gave it to Rid, who snatched it out of his hand and then spat it out when he found it wasn't chicken.

"Oh, so you're not so hungry after all, Mr. Particular Ridiculous?"

But Rid sat up again. His passionate longing for a piece of chicken shone from the melting brown eyes that fixed Jo's blue ones.

"Oh, all right!" said Jo, resignedly parting with a slice of chicken. Rid gulped it avidly. "Listen, you," said Jo, "Freedle gives you a huge meal at night and you are only supposed to eat once a day. I'm a person and I'm supposed to have three meals."

The remarks didn't cut any ice with Rid, but when he saw that the chicken sandwiches were gone he wandered off to hunt for chipmunks.

While Jo munched on brownies between bites of apple, he looked out over the pond. Shimmering butterfly wings of light danced on the ripples flipped up by a passing breeze.

"Gosh, it's pretty here," he thought, and ran his hand through his hair in a gesture he had picked up from Gramp. "How can they call this Ghostly Pond, I wonder?"

He stuffed the apple core and the half carrot he had saved for Quicksie into the pocket of his blue jeans. "Better get to work," he decided. "Gramp will have a fit if he comes back and finds I haven't done anything."

Dip, slap, slap, slap; dip, slap, slap, slap. The

paint flowed on smoothly as he brushed back and forth with even strokes. How long did paint take to dry? As the work began to be monotonous his mind wandered from the happy new place in which he found himself back into the dark miserable world of his own troubles. He began to think about his mother. She'd gone off to Hawaii to marry this man, who was now his stepfather, because the man couldn't leave his job there. He had some big deal on or something.

Anyway, Jo had never even seen the guy. But he hated him. Slap, slap, slap went the paintbrush in Jo's hand. Yes, he hated him and his own father too. People were no good. He hated people. Did he hate Gramp? Well, Gramp was different. Gramp just sort of told you about things and how to do them. That was pretty good. And Gran, what about Gran? She seemed to like him. He liked people to like him, really. Why hadn't his father liked him? His mother liked him; maybe she even loved him. He loved her. But she had gone off to marry this guy he had never seen. He remembered her hand on his hair. "Your hair is the color of your mother's," people often had told him. His mother's hair was pale, golden yellow and he guessed his was about the same. If that guy who had married his mother was here he'd paint him all over red and sock him in the eye.

Jo was distracted from these unpleasant thoughts by the reappearance of Rid, who flung himself down on the ground beside him and lay there panting with weariness. The long hound tail gave a weak thump of recognition as Jo reached out his hand to pat him.

"Well, Rid, I guess I've done all the painting I can do until this dries and I can turn her over. Let's both take a rest, boy, eh?" And Jo stretched out on his back beside the pond where thickly-fallen pine needles made a natural resting place. Rid shifted his head onto Jo's stomach and went to sleep with a sigh of contentment. Jo softly smoothed his long, cool ears.

Looking up, Jo saw a paint-box blue sky and clouds that looked like creamy, whipped desserts spooned into mounds by some giant hand. The sun felt lovely and warm. Beside him the water lapped the shore with a slow *clap-po-ti* sound, very soothing, very liquid. The dog's head on his stomach was warm and comforting. Jo dozed. He dreamed all his class in school was visiting him and he was cooking lunch for them in his cabin. There didn't seem to be enough eggs, in spite of the fact that Rid kept racing in with eggs in his mouth and dropped them beside Jo. Because it was a dream, it seemed natural that the eggs didn't break. "Send Quicksie to buy bacon," he called to someone. But horses don't have money, he suddenly remembered. Everything was getting very difficult and confused.

"Hey, wake up, Jo!" It was Gramp's voice laughing and calling to him. He opened his eyes and saw his grandfather standing over him. Rid was wagging his tail—he hadn't barked at the familiar footsteps.

"Time to push off. You've done a good job, I see."

Rubbing his eyes, Jo got stiffly to his feet and felt in his pocket for the piece of carrot and apple core he had saved for Quicksie.

"How long does it take for paint to dry?" he asked.

"Oh, about twenty-four hours. You can come back tomorrow and finish the job."

"Great!" said Jo. "I want to get her in the water."

# 6

"Well, I guess the ghost was here last night," announced Gramp cheerfully at breakfast one morning late in June. "Just took a walk on the lawn and the same old window was open."

Gran glanced at him, and it was hard for Jo to tell what her expression meant.

"I'm not sure I'm as fond of ghosts as you are," she said softly.

It was difficult for Jo to keep from loving Gran. She was so quiet and kind. Often when she found something amusing in a magazine she would leave it on the desk in his room with the corner of a page turned down. Always she was interested to hear anything he wanted to tell her about Rid or Quicksie. But although Gran never made demands on him, Jo still held aloof. Something hard and cold surrounded his heart and would not melt.

Gramp was helping himself to sausages and eggs. "What harm does a ghost do?" he asked. "Come on up with me after breakfast, Jo, and we'll have a look round. Did you hear anything unusual, Freedle?"

Shrugging her huge shoulders, Freedle replied, "Sheep baaing out on the lawn, Mr. Shaw, but they do that every night."

With mingled dread and excitement, Jo followed his grandfather upstairs and they paused in front of the door that Freedle had shown him on the night he arrived.

"Whose room is this?" he asked.

"No one's," replied Gramp, turning the door handle. "It's an upstairs sitting room that's never used."

As he pushed the door open, an unmistakable smell of violets blew into their faces.

"Hmm!" said Gramp and knitted his brows. "Now let's think this thing through. You have had nothing to do with this because it's happened several times before you arrived. I know your grandmother is just as puzzled as I am; and as for Freedle, she can't move down this corridor without sounding like a ten-ton truck in motion, so that's out."

Jo peered around the corner of the door. The small sitting room was lined with bookcases. Faded blue hangings matched the rug. One of the windows was open and the curtains floated gently out on the morning breeze.

"Maybe someone came with a ladder and opened the window from outside," speculated Jo.

"No, that's impossible," said Gramp. "These are French windows. They crank open from the inside. What do you make of the smell of violets?" he asked Jo.

"Perhaps it smells like that all the time," surmised Jo.

"No, it doesn't," said Gramp.

"Maybe there's a bed of violets outside the window," Jo suggested.

"No, there isn't," Gramp replied. "Anyway, this happened once last January and you don't get violets blooming in the snow."

"I'll tell you what I choose to think," said Gramp. "I choose to think it's a real ghost. This house is quite old. We never changed parts of it when we bought it. Take this sitting room for instance: all the books, the rug, and even the curtains were here when we bought it. And you know, this place has had a rather sad history. Shortly after we bought the house, your grandmother found some old letters in the attic. One of them told about a tragic parting that took place in this very room. A young girl whose family owned the house said farewell to her fiancé. He kissed her good-by in this sitting room and gave her a bunch of violets. Then he went to war and was killed. As he left her forever she leaned out the window and waved good-by."

"The window that's open?" wondered Jo. His eyes were dark with excitement, and the freckles stood out on his pale face.

"Yes," said Gramp. "The letter told how she had waved good-by to him through the north window."

"North, yes," said Jo, "yes, that's north. The sun rises over here," and he indicated with his right hand the east. "Gosh!" he said and looked inquiringly at Gramp.

"Well," said Gramp, "I think it's all very romantic and sad and beautiful. Let's leave it at that. Come on," he said practically, "I want to get you doing a little low jumping today. Your riding has improved amazingly in the few weeks you've been here."

As they came out the front door they saw Gran in the rose garden. She was pushing a light mower down one of the grass paths between the rose beds. The mower whirled a little cloud of fresh, green confetti into the air and continued the musical turning of its blades even after Gran stopped it at the path's edge.

"No new discoveries?" she asked. Gramp shook his head.

Jo looked back at the big vine-covered house which harbored a young girl's ghost, or so Gramp chose to think. Jo felt differently. He didn't say anything, but he decided to keep his eyes open.

Gramp talked about music as they walked toward the stable. He and Gran were practicing a new piece for violin and piano.

"I think it would be fun if you learned to play the flute, Jo," said Gramp. "Come on, I'll start teaching you tonight. Oh, no, I can't," he remembered. "We have a couple of people coming for supper, and I believe you're eating early in the kitchen with Freedle. But tomorrow night," he urged, "how about it?"

"I'll have a try sometime," answered Jo noncommittally.

"Yes, do," encouraged Gramp. "It's a lot of fun and you might get to be really good, you know."

The lilacs beside the lane had long since faded. "I must cut off the dead heads," said Gramp, picking one and tossing it on the ground. "Clean your horse and then saddle up," he directed as he slid open the stable door. "I'm just going to have a look at the oats. I think a rat's been in the bin."

Quicksie was in her stall and Jo called her by name. Oh, his beautiful mare! Jo's heart was full of pride and love as he cleaned her and put on her saddle and bridle.

Rid, who by now was Jo's shadow, sat on the stable floor and watched Jo work. He wagged his tail from time to time in anticipation of the ride.

Quicksie lowered her head so Rid could lick her nose while Jo combed her black tail.

"I guess you're a couple of friends," said Jo, and he gave first one, then the other, a pat.

"What a boring sort of life I used to lead when we lived in that ranch house!" thought Jo. "But gosh, the hotel was even worse!" He pulled up the girth and checked the throat latch of the bridle to see that it wasn't too tight. Yes, he knew he was lucky. Now he had miles of country and woods all around, and nobody told him not to do things. Gran and Gramp seemed to take it for granted that life was such wonderful fun that anyone with any sense would naturally use his wits to stay alive.

The second time they went over to the pond,

Gramp had asked him whether he knew how to swim. It was the day Jo finished painting the boat. Gramp had sat on Trumpet by the pond and watched Jo dive a couple of times and swim back to the little dock.

"Guess you had a pretty good teacher at the Y pool," was all he had said.

The mare would be ready to go after Jo had picked out her feet. (He'd forgotten to clean her feet when he had brought her in yesterday.) He took a hoof pick out of his pocket and cleaned bits of straw and gravel from around the frog. He found one good-size stone that might have made her go lame.

"Come on, Quicksie!" He led her outside and swung himself lightly into the saddle. What a difference from the first day! Now he could get on and off as easily as breathing.

Gramp appeared in the doorway and smiled approvingly. "Good job!" he said. "I'll meet you in the big field where the jumps are. You can leave the gate open. Nothing's turned out there," and he went back into the stable to saddle Trumpet.

Horses should be walked for about a quarter of a mile before trotting to get the circulation going gently. Start them slowly and bring them in cool; that was something Jo had learned. He dismounted to open the gate. Quicksie had a good deal to learn about being a gate horse, and this gate swung so it wasn't a good one to train her on. Jo loved getting on and off, and the mare was patient about standing for him.

He decided after a few minutes that he'd walked long enough and began to trot slowly around the field. Gramp joined him.

"We'll trot over these low jumps first," he said presently. "Follow me, lean forward, keep your heels down, grip with your knees, and three strides before the jump give her her head. I want you to grab a piece of her mane so you won't snatch her mouth before you learn to stick tight!"

"Let's go!" And Gramp trotted off.

Trumpet rose smoothly in his stride and was over the jump. Following along behind, Jo grabbed a piece of Quicksie's mane and then felt a lovely breathlessness as the mare left the ground and cleared the pole without a touch.

"Oh, boy, that's great!" he thought. "And here we go again!" It was like flying.

Gramp laughed when he turned around and saw Jo's beaming face. "I guess you are a natural horseman," he said. "Let's do it at a canter."

Whee, this was even better—what a thrill! He knew he wasn't sticking any too tight to the saddle when he landed and he vowed he'd practice every day and get better. He understood why Gramp wanted him to hang on to a piece of Quicksie's mane.

"Well, that's enough for today," pronounced Gramp. "I'll walk my horse until he is cool and then I've got to get back to the house. What are you going to do?"

"I guess I'll ride up the drive," said Jo, "and ask Freedle to put some lunch in my saddlebag. I'm going over to the pond."

"Well, pick up the knapsack at the stable and put some oats in it for your mare. The grass must be pretty well eaten out of that corral and you are giving her so much work nowadays she should be getting at least six quarts of oats a day. You fed her two this morning along with her hay and you'll feed her two tonight. Another two at noontime will be good for her. A horse should eat little and often. Don't forget to water her before she eats, but be sure she's cool. Well, enjoy yourself. I'll just keep Trumpet walking around here for a few minutes."

Back at the stable Jo filled the knapsack with oats. He noticed some rat droppings on the floor near the oat bin. He guessed that was what Gramp had been talking about.

"Come on, Rid, let's go," he called as he swung up onto the mare's back. The dog led the way, tail up like a proud flag, long ears swinging. They jogged gently up the drive under the shade of the big trees and round to the kitchen door.

Sitting loosely in the saddle, he cupped his hand so his voice would carry. "Freedle," he called, "could I please have some lunch? I'm going to the pond."

The words were no sooner out of his mouth than he found himself flying through the air,

95

and the next thing he knew he was lying in a large bush beside the kitchen door.

With a panicky clatter of little hoofs, sheep that had been grazing around the corner of the house raced down the drive.

Quicksie was trotting away, reins dangling.

"What happened?" Jo picked himself up. Without warning, the mare had suddenly swung to the left and sent him flying.

The sheep! That was it. First Quicksie had scared the sheep, then the sheep had scared Quicksie. All of them had scared Jo.

His horse—he must catch his horse; he didn't want Gramp to see her going riderless back to the stable.

She was slowing up to a walk. Jo gave the whistle he always used to call her to him.

Just then unexpected help arrived in the form of Rid, who had run ahead of Quicksie and now stood facing her barking. The mare stopped, and Jo walked quietly up to her and patted her neck as he caught hold of the reins with his other hand.

"We were all scared," he said. "It wasn't your fault, old girl. Thanks, Rid."

The dog wagged his tail. "Any time I can be of service," he seemed to say.

By the time Jo led his horse back to the kitchen door, Freedle had his lunch bag ready.

"My, but you looked funny!" she exclaimed, her sides shaking with laughter. "Just like a bird you flew, and then boomp in the bush."

Jo wasn't too pleased to be laughed at but was glad to get the lunch, which he fastened to the side of his saddle with a short strap behind the girth.

He looked at Freedle. "It was the sheep," he said briefly. "They scared her. Thanks for the lunch. See you at supper time. I guess I'm going to eat with you. Are you going to make something good—something with cheese, maybe?"

"What I make is always good," said Freedle complacently.

Jo grinned. "Well, see you later," he called over his shoulder.

The sun was warm on his back as he rode

across the field toward the wood. He wondered about having a try at jumping the low snake fence where he usually took down the rails, but his confidence was momentarily shaken by his recent fall, although it hadn't hurt him. He found himself looking for things Quicksie might shy at. The fence was looming closer, and to put off a decision he stopped and dismounted. Looping the reins over his arm, he began to gather the tiny wild strawberries.

Rid lay down in the long grass and panted, his tongue dripping moisture onto his paws.

The blood-red berries flamed like hidden jewels in the grass, which Jo pushed aside with his hand. Ripe and unripe fruit hung on slender, bending stems. As he strolled slowly along, the horse followed after him and snatched mouthfuls of grass.

The glow of partly hidden berries made him think of little stop lights. Jo bent and picked carefully, pulling gently so as not to crush the delicate fruit. His fingers became stained and when he brushed a mosquito from his nose he smelled sun-warmed strawberries. Once he found a tiny, yellow toadstool sheltered by a strawberry plant which hung over it like a miniature tree. He almost saw a little leprechaun sitting on the toadstool throne and imagined him reaching up to pick a strawberry. When Jo's flight of fancy stopped and he returned to himself he felt huge, so entirely had he lost himself in the little scene among the tall grass.

Head down, searching, picking, and eating, he had wandered into a clump of daisies and buttercups near the fence by the wood. The flowers moved responsively to the summer wind. Overhead, tree branches rustled. Jo thought about the wind, how it has no voice but speaks through the sound of rustling leaves, how you can't see it but it is there. The sun lay like a warm hand on his back; his legs were flicked by timothy grass and buttercup stems. Cool little runners of air caressed him and ruffled his hair. His body felt a part of the nature that was all around him. He no longer seemed a boy that nobody wanted. In a way he had never experienced before he belonged to this world of wind and grass and sky and animals; he was in it, and it was in him. He felt contentment and peace.

Ridiculous had followed Jo's slow progress through the grass, wishing no doubt that the juicy bits of red that Jo was finding were morsels of raw meat.

Jo wiped the remains of juice from his fingers onto the mare's gray neck where it made a little pattern. Should he or should he not try that jump on his own? He wished Gramp would give him a few more directions about what he could and could not do. All Gramp had said was, "When you decide to jump, throw your heart over and your horse will follow it. If you feel uncertain, you are asking for a refusal and you will probably get it." Jo didn't want to be chicken, but he just didn't feel like taking that jump all alone way out here. Suddenly a solution occurred to him which saved his self-respect and settled everything. He would let down the bars now, but on the way home he would undoubtedly jump it.

In the wood it was cool and birds sang pleasant songs in different voices. The stream that had rushed through the wood with such a babble and a gurgle in May was quieter and shallower. The mare picked her way delicately across, her feet making liquid plops in the water. Rid took the opportunity to lie down and cool off for a moment. He drank with laps of his tongue as the water trickled past him.

Jo did not allow Quicksie to drink because once when he did she had started to paw and lie down. He had had to give her an awful wallop with his legs to get her going that day, and he remembered all too well how he had almost had an unexpected swim.

"Push on, old girl!" he said. "I'll give you a nice bucket of water when we get to the cabin," and he pressed his legs strongly against her sides. "Come on, slow poke!" he called to Rid.

They emerged from the cool, ferny wood. Ahead of him he saw a steep hill covered with a fleece of daisies which blended with a low-lying cloud.

Out in the sunshine Jo had to slap at the flies that settled on the mare's sweaty neck. He turned left away from the hill and skirted the wood at a slow jog. It was good and hot, and he looked forward to a swim and a row in the red boat. Perhaps he would take Rid with him and eat his lunch out in the middle of the water.

As they approached the cabin, Rid began to sniff and the hair on his back rose up. From time to time he stiffened and growled.

"What's the matter, boy?" asked Jo uneasily. "Smell a bear?" As soon as he had said the word, he wished he hadn't even thought of such a thing.

When Jo took the saddle and bridle off Quicksie, she had a good roll on the short grass of the corral. She was sweaty still, although he had walked her along the path skirting the pond. He decided it was the very hot day and brought her half a bucket of water with the thought that he'd get her more later.

What was the matter with Rid? What had gotten into him? He stood sniffing at the cabin door and growling softly, his hair bristling along the ridge of his back.

Suddenly Jo felt a very long way away from everybody. The pine trees around the cabin sighed softly in the gentle wind; the water of the pond lapped the shore. With a flash of red, a cardinal swooped past on rapid wings as jewel-like as the berries Jo had been peacefully picking a short time ago.

Without letting his imagination dwell any more on silly things like bears, Jo called quaveringly to Rid. "Come on, old boy! Come and find that chipmunk in the cabin." He needed all the support his dog could give him as he gave the cabin door a push. As the hinges groaned and squeaked like something alive, Jo stepped into the damp, musty-smelling room—and froze!

# 7

A boy about his age or a little older was standing with his back to the fireplace, looking at him defiantly.

"What are you doing here?" asked Jo, taking a step backward.

"What are *you* doing?" retorted the boy in a surly voice. His black, angry eyes glared at Jo under heavy brows. His wiry hair needed cutting and stood as stiff and dark as the mane of an animal.

104

"This is my grandfather's cabin!" declared Jo, with what firmness he could muster.

"Call your dog back before I kick him," said the boy. Rid was not acting very friendly, for he sensed Jo's uneasiness.

"Come on outside and tell me who you are," said Jo, and he backed out the door, pulling Rid along by the collar.

To Jo's relief and surprise, the boy obeyed and followed him through the door. Rid had quieted down and sat at Jo's command.

"What are you doing here? You're trespassing, you know." When he got a good look at the intruder, Jo felt a little surer of himself, for the face before him was thin and pale and the eyes suddenly seemed more scared than angry.

"What if I told you? You'd go tell the cops, wouldn't you?"

"The police! Gosh, are they after you?" asked Jo incredulously.

"Sure," said the boy. Then he questioned him roughly, "Got any food?"

"Why?" asked Jo foolishly. "Are you hungry?"

"Just about starving," said the boy. "I haven't eaten nothing but strawberries for three days and there wasn't many of them."

Jo looked at him and knew he spoke the truth. "Wait a minute," he said.

In no time he was back with his well-stuffed bag of lunch. The boy's black eyes had followed his every movement like an animal.

"Sit down," said Jo. "Here's some food."

Freedle had packed a lunch of roast beef sandwiches, hard-boiled eggs, and an apple tart and cheese.

Like a wolf, the boy swallowed an egg, hardly chewing it at all.

"Don't eat so fast. You'll be sick," said Jo, staring at him.

The boy shot him a look that seemed to say, "What do you care if I'm sick or not?"

Although Jo had often felt good and hungry before a meal, he had never been hungry like this. He looked curiously at the boy sitting on the ground and knew he was seeing someone who was literally starving. To his surprise, his advice was taken and the boy ate a roast beef sandwich, chewing the bites deliberately.

"You'd better save some for supper," Jo remarked prudently.

"Yeah." The boy nodded his dark head in agreement.

"What's your name?" asked Jo, changing the subject. It was rather hard to watch his lunch disappearing like that. He was hungry himself.

"Tony," answered the boy briefly.

"Where did you come from?" asked Jo. He was now more curious than frightened.

"Black Hill Reform School," Tony replied tersely.

"Oh," said Jo, "you escaped." He sat down hard on a log, and they stared at one another while Tony continued to eat.

"Going to tell on me?" asked the boy, half threatening, half pleading.

"No," said Jo. Then, after a pause, "What did you do? Why did they put you in there?"

"Killed someone," said Tony.

Jo moved uneasily. If he'd heard the boy sitting before him declare himself a murderer when he'd first seen him inside the cabin, he would have been good and scared. But now that he'd saved him from starvation, he had a proprietary feeling about him.

"Why did you do it?" asked Jo. "Did you belong to a gang?"

"No," said Tony. He looked hard at Jo. "I hit

my stepfather over the head with a chair. He died."

"Oh," said Jo. Something uncomfortable was happening inside him. A train of pictures was flashing through his mind—his mother, his father, his stepfather, whose unknown face he had so often punched in imagination.

"Why?" he asked faintly.

"Because he was beating up my mother again," said Tony.

"Oh," remarked Jo. "I guess you did right," he added, trying to persuade himself.

"Well, they said I shouldn't have killed him. I hit him too many times. I got real mad."

"No, I suppose you shouldn't have killed him," agreed Jo uncomfortably.

"They sent me up for four years. Got to learn to control my temper." Tony laughed bitterly.

"What are you going to do? Why did you escape?"

"There I guess I made a mistake," said Tony. He looked longingly at the tart and then put it in the pocket of his loose, shabby, brown trousers.

"I got a chance to beat it when a guard wasn't looking and I lit out. I just couldn't take it there."

"What did they do to you?" asked Jo eagerly.

"Oh, nothing much," said Tony noncommittally.

"But what are you going to do now?" Jo looked curiously at Tony.

"You tell me," replied the boy bitterly.

Jo sat for some time looking thoughtful. It didn't seem to occur to Tony that Jo might be hungry. "Got to give my horse some more water and feed her," he remarked finally.

When he returned he found Tony lying on his back, his hands clasped behind his head, looking up at the sky.

"There's a cloud up there that looks like a big cat. See what I mean?" asked Tony.

Jo eased down on the ground beside him and gazed up at the cloud formations drifting by. "I see it," he said. "But look. Now it's changing into a ship."

"Yeah," said Tony, "I see it." After a minute he rolled over on his side and looked at Jo. "I've

110

always lived in the city—New York. I've never laid down on the ground before. I never seen nothing like this before except in pictures," and he waved his hand vaguely in the direction of the pond, the woods and the fields.

"Do you have a nice house?" asked Jo tentatively.

"House!" Tony laughed bitterly. "Two rooms for the family and ten flights of stairs to get there. We live on the Lower East Side. Ever hear of it?"

"No," said Jo. "I'm going for a swim," he decided suddenly, and started pulling off his clothes.

"If I went in the water I'd drown," said Tony. He saw Jo dive off the dock and come to the surface shaking his head and blowing water out of his nose. There was envy in his eyes as he watched Jo churn his way through the water in an expert crawl.

Jo lay on his back and floated and pondered. What should Tony do? What could he do to help him? Bring him food, that was the first thing.

Somehow he had to get some extra food and not let Gran or Gramp or Freedle know what he needed it for.

Presently he swam ashore and started to dress. He wanted to ask Tony a lot of questions about reform school, but he didn't.

"You've got a blanket on the bunk in the cabin," he said.

"Yeah," said Tony listlessly.

"I'll come back tomorrow and bring you more food."

Tony gave him a quick look of astonishment, then a nervous look of gratitude. "You will?" he asked unbelievingly.

"I promise," said Jo.

Tony stared at him. "I ate your lunch," he said.

"That's all right," said Jo, whose stomach was growling with hunger. "Don't worry about me. I'll get a big supper." He thought of the kitchen where Freedle would heap his plate.

"Want to watch me saddle up?" he asked.

"I guess so," said Tony.

112

They walked to the corral together, Rid staying close to Jo as if to protect him from this stranger about whom he still felt uncertain. "You ain't afraid of horses, are you?" the boy asked admiringly.

"Nothing to be afraid of," said Jo nonchalantly as he tightened up Quicksie's girth.

When he swung into the saddle he felt like a Pony Express rider. This outpost depended on him and his horse to bring supplies. "So long," he called, waving his hand, and trotted off along the path. He knew he shouldn't start off trotting, but he couldn't imagine the Pony Express starting off at a slow walk.

All the way home he thought about Tony. Tomorrow he would ask him a lot of questions about reform school.

Because Jo felt useful he was momentarily light-hearted. He forgot the guilty feelings that Tony had awakened in him. At school Jo had heard a teacher say, "There but for the grace of God go I." Suddenly this afternoon, while he was talking to Tony, he had understood what

113

that sentence meant. However, the fact that he himself had only *thought* of violence, not *committed* it, made him temporarily light-hearted. In contrast to Tony's background of poverty and stupidity he couldn't help feeling superior. This place was his family's—his grandfather's and grandmother's. He belonged—if not to a mother and father, at least to grandparents.

When he finally came to the low snake fence at the edge of the wood, he faced his mare squarely at it, urged her to a canter, hung onto her mane, threw his heart over and sailed into the field beyond. Riding Quicksie on a loose rein, he continued to canter on through the daisies and buttercups and over strawberry plants, which he supposed he was squashing.

The mares, who had been grazing in the adjoining field, moved down the fence line with him. Alongside their dams the foals jumped into the air and then gave little bucks from good spirits.

Jo laughed aloud to see them so gay. They were growing bigger and stronger every day.

He looked back to make sure Rid was following. "Come on, slow poke," he called. "Come on, Ridiculous! We're nearly home."

But when he walked Quicksilver up the drive toward the house his mood changed. All sorts of doubts and fears assailed him. Aside from his worries about what he should do to help Tony, a thought that for weeks had been kept in the background suddenly came into sharp focus. That first day at Strawberry Hill his grandfather had said, "If you get along well with the mare, she is yours." What had he meant by that? Was she really his, or just for him to ride? Was it possible his grandfather might sell her?

The colts Gramp raised were sold for big prices as race horses. He found that out by listening to people who came to Strawberry Hill. What if Quicksie herself could run very fast and someone wanted to buy her? Would Gramp sell her? Or did he mean it that she really belonged to him? He wanted desperately to ask, but was so afraid to hear the answer he didn't dare.

If he could just know that Quicksie couldn't gallop fast he would feel better, but he didn't dare find out the truth and had never let her go as fast as she could.

Every day he loved the beautiful mare more. He and she were almost like two pieces of a jigsaw puzzle; they got on well together, all right, there was no doubt about that.

# 8

Freedle was stirring something in a pot on the stove. A big, blue apron covered her massive stomach and hips, and her crown of yellow braids surmounted a face bright pink from the heat of the kitchen. To Jo, who had not eaten anything more than a few strawberries since breakfast, the cooking smelled incredibly delicious.

"What are you making?" he asked.

"Sauce for the chicken and noodles," replied

Freedle, and suddenly her fat sides began to shake with laughter. The sound of Jo's voice had recalled the events of the morning. "Boomp in the bush! Ha, ha, ha!" she chortled.

"Yes, yes, very funny," said Jo rather sourly. "When's supper?" he asked.

"I give you yours in half an hour," said Freedle, tasting from the spoon and then adding a little salt to the pot.

Jo sat down and watched her as she lumbered over to a cupboard and searched inside. "No sugar. Get me some out of the storeroom, Jo. That's right," she directed. "I need some for the whipped-cream chocolate pudding."

"You mean in here?" asked Jo, as he put his hand tentatively on a doorknob at the far end of the big, old-fashioned kitchen.

"Ya, ya, in there," Freedle replied impatiently.

The inside of the storeroom was dark, but the light from the kitchen showed a string hanging from an overhead light. He pulled it, and in the brightness of the unshaded bulb, he looked around at Freedle's kingdom of mops and

118

brushes, pails and stepladders and ironing boards. There were all sorts of jutting angles and big cupboards and shelves; the place seemed as large as a bedroom. How was he to know where she kept the sugar? He saw bins of vegetables and boxes of various things on the shelves.

Her voice drifted in to him. "The door with the red knob—straight ahead."

He pulled open the cupboard door and saw a big canister marked *sugar*, which he hauled out and lugged into the kitchen.

"Thanks," said Freedle. "You want to eat, you work. Sit down there," she added, indicating a table with a couple of chairs beside it.

"Freedle," said Jo coaxingly as he sat down, "give me a few boxes of crackers or something. I want to have extra supplies at the cabin. I might get hungry or have to stay late or something." He hoped he was sounding natural.

Freedle looked at him sharply. "I give you plenty food in your lunch bag. What you want to do, run away from home?"

This hit a little too close to the mark, and Jo protested violently. "Why should I want to run away? Don't be silly. I just said I wanted some more food."

"I give you an extra sandwich tomorrow then. But why are you so hungry right now? You want to know when is supper. Why? Didn't I give you the great big lunch?" She looked curiously at him, and, to his relief, her mind changed course.

"You know," she said, "you and me, we are rare—not many blonds nowadays. Most people got black or brown hair. Your mother, is she blond?" Freedle patted her golden braids and looked inquisitively at Jo, who winced under her gaze. He did not want to talk about his mother, and anyway, her soft golden hair was not at all like Freedle's brassy, gold braids.

"You got freckles," said Freedle. "On your nose you got freckles."

The evening paper was lying on the table and Jo, wishing Freedle would stop being so personal, reached for it and opened it up.

"What's the headlines?" asked Freedle as she returned to stirring the pot of sauce.

Jo's blue eyes opened wide and his face became rather pale, but the fat back turned to him was oblivious of his astonishment.

"Go on, read!" commanded Freedle. "I cook, you read the news."

The paper rustled in Jo's shaking hand, and his voice sounded strained as he read stutteringly.

"Police search for young slayer—reform school escapee still at large."

"Ach!" cried Freedle dropping the spoon. "I knew it would happen someday. One of them bad boys loose. Where's Ridiculous? Come here, come here—we need a watchdog. Poe sloke, poe sloke, where are you?"

Jo had gotten a grip on himself.

"You mean slow poke," he said firmly. "Anyway, he's just outside keeping cool on the doormat."

Freedle drew a gasping breath and remembered her duty. With a shaking hand she opened the oven door and pulled out a little baking dish. Whatever happens, a cook must not let the supper burn.

She set the dish in front of Jo, and the most lovely smell of cheese and bacon and tomatoes rose to his nostrils. The mixture was so hot it seemed to breathe up and down. Waiting for it to cool was almost more than he could endure.

"Gosh, this looks great," he said.

Freedle waddled about the kitchen taking out, putting away, sifting, measuring, doing all the mysterious things people do before a delicious meal appears on the table. She moaned as she worked.

"A murderer hiding in the bushes! My oh my, will I ever see the morning light!"

"I wonder," thought Jo, "what she would say if she knew I had spent the afternoon with him." It made Jo almost laugh, but at the same time he felt sorry for her, she looked so scared.

He began wondering how he was going to get extra food for Tony. Freedle wouldn't give it to him, and he was afraid she locked the store-

room at night. With the terror she had of rob-
bers, he bet she did lock it and kept the key
under her pillow.

Outside the door, Rid whined to be let in.
June bugs were bumping head on into the screen,
then buzzing in an arc of angry frustration before trying another vain assault.

"Hurry up, Rid, come on!" cried Jo as he
held the door open. He didn't want to let the
ugly, brown insects fly past him.

He had been making up his mind to a plan.
When Freedle went into the dining room to serve
Gran and Gramp and their guests he would just
have to swipe some stuff out of the storeroom.
The thought made him feel sick, but what was
he to do? He remembered Tony's pale, hungry
face under its shock of black hair. Jo himself
now knew what it was like to be hungry. Really,
he had felt as ravenous as a wolf before Freedle
had given him that cheese thing. And still he
was waiting anxiously for a good plate of chicken
and noodles while Tony, poor Tony, hadn't
eaten anything but a few berries for three days

until Jo had given him his lunch. Yes, he must steal. He would bide his time.

Ridiculous rested his chin on Jo's knee and looked at his master with loving brown eyes. Jo fingered his dog's long, cool ears.

"When are you going to feed Rid?" he asked.

"There's his dish all ready. Give it to him," said Freedle motioning. "Hot nights he eats better not too early."

A great final bustle of dishing up was going on by the stove.

"Now I take in the food," declared Freedle importantly.

Jo watched her broad back and extended elbows as she carried a platter through the door. Quick as a cat he ran across the kitchen, opened the storeroom door, grabbed a box of crackers and three oranges and dumped them outside the screen door. He was sitting innocently at the table when Freedle lumbered back into the kitchen.

Next time she disappeared he repeated the maneuver and snatched three potatoes and a box of raisins, which joined the crackers and the oranges outside.

Into the kitchen came Freedle. "I think I get a little cool air. Cooking it's hot work," she declared, and started for the screen door.

Jo was horrified and in desperation he cried, "Don't you hear the bell? Gran's calling you back. You forgot something!"

Freedle, who had heard no bell, looked bewildered but started toward the dining room as Jo lit out the screen door. Gathering up his loot as best he could, he made for the stable to put it in his knapsack.

His tack needed cleaning, and by the time he had finished it and fed and watered Quicksie he was tired and decided to go to bed.

Walking back toward the house, he faced full into the sunset where molten-pink clouds seemed like the shores of some fairy, far-off country, and the brilliant bits of blue sky in between had the look of lakes and bays where a boat could sail to an unreal port. He wished he lived in that sky world where he would be able to float on forever in unreality, never having to think about what he should do, never having to worry about people.

As he passed through the house on the way to his room he could hear strange voices and then Gran's laughter. A party. Another party. True it was only the third one since he had come to live with his grandparents at Strawberry Hill. Several times people had dropped in for lunch, and if he wasn't off riding he had eaten with them. But somehow tonight the old left-out feeling returned with renewed force, and he thought, as he had so many times before, "I'm the boy that nobody wants."

Rid seemed to catch his mood and followed him with drooping tail and sagging ears as he opened the door of his room. The intense light of the sinking sun shone strongly on the old racing prints opposite his bed and made them appear more lively than usual. The hobbyhorse poses of the static animals and the cardboard attitudes of their whip-flailing riders suddenly had a sort of charm for him. This was his room,

his sanctuary; here were his books and his things.
He closed the door.

Rid jumped up on the big bed and waited for
Jo to get undressed and join him. The dog kept
looking at the boy, and Jo fancied Rid understood everything. Some of the hardness and
tightness in him began to melt and he flung himself down beside the dog, who licked at Jo's
cheeks where the salt tears tasted good.

"Oh, Rid!" cried the boy in a muffled voice
laying his face against the dog's muzzle. "No-

body wanted you either, did they? Where did you come from? You were hungry and alone and now you're mine."

The light dimmed. In the vines covering the old house the voices of birds quieted into silence. The peeper frogs in the marshes took over the night music. But Jo did not fall asleep.

He lay there thinking. What if Gran and Gramp found out that he was hiding Tony and stealing food? What if they could guess some of the really bad thoughts he had had about his father and his stepfather, and about other things too? Would they still want to keep him? He didn't think so. Then he would have no place to go. If they told him one day, "Jo, you are a bad boy and we don't want you," he would have to creep away quietly in the night. He would take Rid with him, and he would get work somewhere picking vegetables, or maybe being a pin boy in a bowling alley. He and Rid would spend the nights in haystacks. But when winter came, what then? They would freeze outdoors. Besides, he would have to leave Quicksie. He felt caught in

128

a box. Each way his mind went it hit an impossible wall.

Beside him Rid had fallen asleep and in his dreams he was hunting rabbits; his legs jerked as if he were running and he whined eagerly.

The room had become dark. The night wind rustled the leaves of the vine and tapped them against the window sill. He thought of his mother. Would she be sorry if she heard he had frozen to death in a ditch? A few more tears squeezed out of his eyes but Rid was not awake to lick them up.

What if tomorrow someone came by and said he was prepared to pay a lot of money for Quicksie? He felt sick.

When he was a little boy, his Teddy bear had always lain on the pillow beside him and he knew he had a friend. Then one day when he was about six his father had said, "Don't tell me you take that dirty old thing to bed with you still? You must be a real boy now, not a baby." His father had grabbed the bear by one foot and had taken him out of the house and thrown him on a pile of burning leaves. When his fur caught fire, Jo had fancied he heard him squeak and he went behind the garage and was sick.

After that, when he had been left alone while his mother and father went off to a party, he had often tried to comfort himself by pretending he could still feel the bear next to him. But tonight the cool ears of his dog lying against his face made his hand stray to the consolation of something alive next to him. He fell asleep at last, his hand on Rid's head.

# 9

When he opened his eyes the next morning he saw something which, due to his depression and anxiousness, he had not noticed the night before.

Standing in a vase on his desk was a pink rose just beginning to open. Unbelievingly he got out of bed and sniffed it. Beside the flower lay a scrap of paper and he read, "Good night, sleep tight."

So Gran had been thinking of him all along and had given him a rose out of her garden! He sniffed it again and the velvet of the petals stroked his nose.

When he went down, she had already finished her breakfast and had gone outdoors. A little later on, returning to his room to get a hoof pick he'd forgotten, he looked out the window and saw her pruning a rose tree that grew near the front door.

All at once Jo noticed a black sedan coming up the drive to Strawberry Hill. It stopped at the front door and a couple of men got out.

Listening, hidden behind the heavy curtain of his window, Jo heard Gran say, "Good morning," and saw her stand quietly. Her head was tilted attentively as she paid attention to what they had to say.

"Have you seen a boy around her?" asked one of the men, who wore a dark hat pulled down so far on his head that his ears stuck out sideways.

"Just my grandson," replied Gran cheerfully.

"What color is his hair?" asked the other man, who wore a red shirt and had a stupid look about him.

Gran laughed. "He has fair hair. Why?"

"The boy we're looking for has black hair," replied the man. "He's escaped," he added.

"Oh, yes," said Gran, and her voice sounded sad. "I read about it in the paper."

"You haven't seen him?" repeated the man with the dark hat.

"No," said Gran decisively, "I haven't."

"If he's in the woods he's bound to come out soon," said the red-shirted man. "He must be starving."

"I haven't seen him," said Gran briefly. "Good morning," she added and, turning on her heel, walked lightly back into the house.

Jo's heart was pounding. As he watched the car drive away he bit his nails. He wished he could tell Gran about Tony. The situation was weighing heavily on his mind but he could not betray him. For one thing, it would be almost like giving himself up because in some way he felt *he* was Tony; he had the same bad thoughts. The only difference was he hadn't carried them through. Jo was all mixed up. He needed someone to tell him just what he should do. Could he trust Gran or Gramp? If he told them, would they tell the police? He couldn't chance it; he must just keep on taking food to the cabin and hope some solution would turn up.

As he moved from the window he saw his own reflection in the eagle-topped mirror and was surprised at how pale and worried he appeared. "I must be careful. Someone may notice something," he thought, and forced a smile that looked more like a grimace of pain.

It seemed imperative to get over to the cabin quickly and tell Tony what he had just seen and heard.

An hour later he was riding through the woods, the stolen provisions and Quicksie's oats slung on his back.

When he arrived, Tony was at the cabin door to meet him but shrank back into the shelter of the room to keep well away from Quicksie, of whom he was obviously terrified, and from Rid, who wasn't acting very friendly.

"They're after you, Tony," said Jo. "I saw them. Wait till I put my horse in the corral and I'll tell you about it. Come here, Rid," he called to the dog, who was growling and walking stiff-legged toward the door.

"Who did you see? What did they look like?" asked Tony urgently when Jo came back carrying the knapsack which he dropped on the ground inside the cabin.

"One had ears that stuck out," said Jo.

"Yeah, that's Bill the Butch," said Tony, and he wriggled uncomfortably.

"Then there was another man—kind of stupid-looking and wearing a red shirt." Jo looked at Tony to see whether he recognized the description.

"I know who he is." Tony grimaced. "That's Harold. I don't believe he's ever washed that shirt—it stinks.

"You didn't tell on me?" he asked, suddenly both threatening and anxious.

"No, I didn't and I'm not going to!" declared Jo stoutly.

Tony relaxed. "What you got in there?" he asked, indicating the knapsack.

"Take a look," said Jo. "It's all for you. Except the sandwiches," he added quickly. "But

—" He hesitated. "I'll give you some of those too. We'll eat lunch together."

"I don't think I dare go outside," said Tony. He had found the box of raisins and was eating them in handfuls. "Bill the Butch and Harold might come snooping around."

"Let's roast these potatoes," suggested Jo.

"O.K.," agreed Tony. "Do you know how to build a fire?"

"Sure," said Jo, who had learned the hard way after several tries during the past weeks.

He crumpled up one of the sandwich papers in the center of the fireplace and on it crisscrossed a few dry sticks and chips of wood that he had collected one day.

"Light that," he said to Tony, handing him a match and indicating the laid fire. "I'll go outside and get some more wood."

"It's going to be kind of hot in here," said Tony when Jo came back with an armful of wood and laid a few more pieces on the fire. For a moment it looked as if everything was going to go out, but the fire flared up again and began to burn brightly.

136

Jo looked at Tony. "Don't you think we could sit just outside?" he asked. "We can keep an eye out for anyone coming and my dog will growl if he hears something. Come here, Rid!" he called. "Stick around and be a watchdog—you don't have to hunt all the time." Rid came bounding up expectantly, not knowing just what he was supposed to do.

"O.K.," agreed Tony. "We'll go out but we've got to keep watching."

As they sat with their backs against the cabin wall, Jo hooked a finger through Rid's collar.

"When are you going to cook the spuds?" asked Tony.

"We have to let the fire burn down and get a bed of ashes first," said Jo, who had read about this method of cooking potatoes and hoped it would work.

Tony's face was pale and spotty beneath his shock of black hair and he kept moving around and scratching himself.

"Nervous, I guess," thought Jo. Being a hunted fugitive gave Tony a sort of importance in Jo's eyes. To make himself interesting to Tony,

137

Jo said suddenly, "We have a ghost at our house."

"Yeah?" queried Tony, visibly impressed.

"Only I don't think it really is a ghost," said Jo.

"No?" said Tony listlessly, and Jo realized he had lost status by his admission.

"What was it like at that reform school?" he blurted out suddenly.

"Awful," answered Tony briefly.

"What did they do to you?" asked Jo. "Did they beat you up or something?"

"Bill the Butch sometimes did," answered Tony resentfully. "They're not supposed to hit you, but they do."

"Did you have a room of your own?" asked Jo, his eyes wide with curiosity.

"No, of course not," said Tony, scornful of Jo's ignorance. "You sleep all together on a lot of cots. I had a guy next to me who was real tough. He'd stole a car and held up a gas station. He tried to get me to steal some cigarettes for him from Harold. He said if I didn't, he'd do it and say it was me. That was one reason I run away—I was scared of that guy next to me. He told me if I didn't steal them cigarettes from Harold he'd stick a knife in me while I was asleep and say it was another guy done it."

"What did they give you to eat?" asked Jo curiously.

"Oh, I don't know, stew and stuff." His dull face brightened suddenly. "My ma's a good cook," said Tony. "She makes awfully good spaghetti, especially when we've got enough money to buy meat. When are you going to put them spuds to cook?"

Jo got up, brushed some pine needles off the seat of his blue jeans, and went inside. "The fire's still flaming too much," he called out. "I guess we'd better eat the sandwiches. I'll put the potatoes in later and you can have them for your supper."

"O.K.," agreed Tony. "Ain't you going to swim?" he asked.

"I suppose I might as well," said Jo, who was secretly pleased by the impression his swimming had made on Tony.

"I'll stay by the door so I can duck inside,"

said Tony, settling himself solidly against the wall. "If you see anybody coming, yell 'Fourth of July' and I'll know what you mean."

"I get you," said Jo, who set out to impress Tony by staying underwater, blowing water spouts and churning up the pond.

The swim made him feel great, but when he came out, he was annoyed to find that Tony had eaten a lot of the sandwiches without waiting for him. He didn't say anything, but he got ready to leave soon after putting the potatoes to roast in the hot ashes.

Tony could see he was sore and asked, "Will you promise to come back tomorrow?"

"Tomorrow or next day," Jo answered him curtly. "You've got some crackers and oranges left."

Keeping a tree between him and the horse, Tony watched anxiously as Jo mounted. "You'll come back?" he questioned again.

"I'll come back," said Jo as he turned Quicksie's head toward home. "I'll come back," he repeated, but he didn't wave good-by.

When he arrived at Strawberry Hill, he gave Quicksie a workout over the jumps.

"Gosh, I'd like to let her really gallop someday," he thought wistfully. "I'll bet she can go." But if he ever made up his mind to it, he'd be careful that no one was watching. Unfortunately the only flat piece where he could really let her run was well within the view of anyone who might be coming up the drive.

A couple of weeks ago he'd asked Gramp how old Quicksie was, hoping in that way to open up a conversation and get some information about whether he'd ever thought of selling her.

"She's five," Gramp had told him, and said no more.

Jo raised the jump bars to three feet and the mare sailed them with room to spare. He wished Gramp had been watching.

The boy and the horse understood each other very well now. Quicksie had learned to respond to Jo's leg pressures to such an extent that he scarcely needed reins, and they often played a game out in this field. She loved the game as much as he did. It consisted of his guiding her at a trot around various obstacles and not letting her know till the last minute which way she was to go. He could feel her under him, obedient and ready to turn any way he might indicate. She became as agile and balanced as a cat with all the twisting and turning he required of her.

But today he didn't have the gaiety in him to enjoy the game. Letting the reins lie loose on her neck, he walked her in a circle awhile until she was cool. Then he went in and unsaddled.

Something was lying on the bench in the tack room where Gramp must have known Jo would find it.

It was a brightly colored post card showing waves and palm trees. He turned it over and read *Having a wonderful time—wish you were here. Love, Mother.*

"Like fun she does!" said Jo aloud, and he gave the wall a kick which startled Rid, who had been sitting in a corner watching him hang up his saddle and bridle.

"Sorry, Rid," said Jo, but his voice was so glum the dog's ears drooped and his tail gave only a tentative wag to acknowledge the apology.

# 10

Jo didn't go over to Ghostly Pond the next day but hung about the place.

Gramp must have noticed he was out of sorts for he made a special point of asking him to help him halter-break the foals. Some of the babies were very resistant to being led and gave Jo a workout, so by evening he was good and tired.

"Don't forget about that flute lesson," urged Gramp. "Come on, I'll show you how," and he led Jo, who was too weary to protest, into the big drawing room where the music stands were set up around the piano.

From a leather case he lifted a long silver pipe pierced with holes, placed the instrument across his lips, twiddled his fingers and blew a few sweet notes.

"*Siegfried's* bird," he said. "Look here, just blow as if you were blowing across the top of a bottle." Jo accepted the instrument and blew. A breathy, feeble sound came out. He tried again.

"That's better," said Gramp.

Jo was intrigued. By the time his lesson was over he could play a simple little tune.

"You catch on very quickly," said Gramp. "Pretty soon your grandmother and you and I can make a trio. We'll try some easy pieces first. It will be a lot of fun." Gramp ran his hand through his hair till it stood on end, and Jo caught his enthusiasm.

But later, at bedtime, his troubles came rushing back into his mind. Tony hung like a heavy stone around his neck, dragging him down just when life was bright. Would he always, he wondered, have to get food to Tony? Would every day be a worry from now on? Suppose he just didn't go over to Ghostly Pond again? The thought was very tempting.

But if he were Tony and Tony were he, and he was waiting, starving, listening for the thud of a horse's hoofs along the path, hoofs that didn't come—no, no, he must go. He knew he must; he had said he would.

The next morning found him absolutely resolved to go at least once again but to wait until around lunch time before starting so that he could grab a few things for Tony from the sideboard, as well as getting his own sandwiches from Freedle.

Perhaps today he would have a talk with Tony and tell him he couldn't go on like this forever, but he was afraid to think of what Tony might say or do. Suppose Tony told him, "Look here, you're just as guilty as I am now; I'm a criminal and you've been hiding me." Suppose he said, "If I'm captured I'll tell the police who has been helping me to hide out." Jo's mind was in a whirl. The day was muggy, and lowering black clouds were building up in the west. As Gramp had said, the land needed rain. As he walked down the drive he had the feeling that everything, every blade of grass, every leaf, every flower, was panting and waiting, listening for the first drops to fall.

Jo stopped by the fence where the mares and foals were grazing. The brown mare, the one he had given a carrot the night he arrived at Strawberry Hill, strolled over to the fence and stretched her neck across, hoping for something special. Luckily he had a piece of sugar in his pocket. Her foal was growing into a strong little creature. The bewildered baby look had left his face and he knew a lot more about the world—how it was a place to gallop and play and then sleep in the grass while his mother stood guard nearby. He came to the fence to make friends and Jo scratched his forehead.

"I'll give you sugar when you're a big boy," he told him. "Did you like your halter lesson yesterday? I think you were one of the good boys."

Rid ran about saying hello to the horses, who

were quite used to him and scarcely paid any attention to him. Suddenly the dog took off on one of his daily rabbit hunts. "Attaboy! Get him!" called Jo. As far as he knew, Rid had never come near catching anything.

Jo had resolved to spend the morning cleaning his tack. As he pushed open the tack room door he thought he heard a funny noise in one of the feed bins, but he paid no special attention for his mind was in such a turmoil that it only dimly registered the world about him. Could you really be arrested for harboring a criminal? Jo thought you could; he remembered something he had once read about such a thing. Besides, he was a thief; he had stolen from his grandparents to give to a murderer and then he had lied to Freedle to make his escape with the loot. Jo felt sick. In his fevered imagination he saw the black car coming up the drive again. He pictured the two men getting out and the one in the red shirt laying a hand on his shoulder. "You are under arrest for harboring a fugitive from the law." After that he supposed he would be shut up in the Black Hill Reform School from which Tony had escaped. Perhaps they would beat him, perhaps he would die there. Then there would be another ghost haunting Strawberry Hill. He was almost sobbing he felt so sorry for himself, so guilty, so miserable. No one wanted him; he was a criminal himself.

Despite these worried thoughts Jo could not help but notice the thumping going on outside the tack room door. He felt too miserable to be scared. What could frighten him now? Nothing. He was sure he wanted to die anyway. His face, if he had been able to see it, had the same sullen look Tony's had had when Jo first found him. He opened the tack room door.

The noise came from one of the tin bins of oats. It was almost empty, and someone, probably Jo himself, had forgotten to put back the lid. He peered inside and saw an enormous rat with flaming eyes and a long, naked tail. As Jo's face looked into the bin, the rat gave another desperate leap to free itself, then fell back onto the oats.

A strange, cruel, hard feeling grew in Jo. This thing was trapped, it was evil, it was at his mercy. He picked up a broom and with the handle he prodded the rat, which leapt and squeaked and snarled at him. For one moment Jo was afraid the rat was going to get out and bite him, and he sprang back. Then he realized that it was impossible for the creature to escape. Again the hot feeling of hatred came over him. He wanted to hurt the rat. He ran outside the stable door and collected a handful of stones. Returning to the barn, he stood beside the barrel and threw a big stone hard at the rat's head. It began to bleed. He threw another—and another. A hot, cruel feeling of wanting to hurt welled up inside him. He was completely absorbed.

"Jo!"

It was as if the voice of God had spoken out of the heavens, and Jo snapped his head up guiltily to see his grandfather standing in the stable door.

They stood and looked at one another. Gramp's face was solemn and stern.

"Come outside," said Gramp quietly.

Jo followed him through the door.

"Move over onto the grass," said Gramp.

Jo saw a look of sorrow, not of anger, on Gramp's face. He dropped his eyes and relaxed his hands so that the stone he still held fell with a thud into the grass.

"I'm only going to say one thing," said Gramp, "and then I'm going to knock you down. The great law of life is love," said Gramp gently. "Hatred and cruelty are sinful." With that he hauled off and hit Jo a blow on the chest that stretched him flat on his back.

He lay there dazed and thought dimly, "I'm glad Rid can't see me; I'm glad he's off hunting rabbits." He heard Gramp go into the stable and knew somehow that he had quickly and mercifully killed the rat.

The long grass half hid him where he lay. He thought he should get up but he didn't seem to want to for a moment. Strangely enough he felt peaceful and happy. His heart, which had been aching with guilt and misery, had suddenly be-

151

come light. He had done wrong and he had been
punished. He felt punished for all his ugly, hate-
ful thoughts toward his stepfather, toward the
rat, toward people in general. He looked up at
the sky and saw Gramp's hand stretched out to
him.

Gramp hauled Jo to his feet and said, "I de-
test what you did, but you know how I feel about
you."

Jo looked into Gramp's eyes and saw love and understanding.

"This is just between us," Gramp said brusquely and, turning abruptly, walked off down the lane.

It was a good many minutes before Jo pushed open the sliding door at the back of the stable and gave his whistle for Quicksie.

The gray mare nudged Jo's pocket impatiently, for he was being slow about giving her the carrot he always handed out as a reward for coming obediently. He buried his head in her black mane, one arm was thrown across her neck and he gave her a loving squeeze.

Quicksie nibbled at his pocket. "Affection is all very nice," she seemed to say, "but what about something practical, like a carrot?"

Jo laughed and handed it to her and listened to the crunch she made as she ate it.

"Are you really mine?" he asked wistfully, running his hand down her neck. "Did Gramp mean, if we got on together, that you really belonged to me, or are you just sort of a loan?

"You're mine, Quicksie," he said, laying his cheek on her neck. "And I'm yours," he added softly.

"Hi, Ridiculous, where have you been?" he asked as the dog came up panting. Jo leaned to stroke the cool ears while the mare put her nose down to be licked. He had one hand on his horse and one on his dog. The three stood there together for a moment.

"I must go back to the stable and clean my tack," said Jo, straightening up. "Good-by, Quicksie! Come on, Rid!"

An hour later Jo went up to the house to get his bagful of lunch at the kitchen door. He left again by way of the rose garden and saw Gran sitting on a bench near her flowers reading a letter.

"Come here a minute, Jo," she called. "Sit down beside me. This letter is for you too."

It was to Gran from his mother, and in it she said that she was very happy and told how good and kind her new husband was. His name was Bob. Written at the end was a special bit for Jo. *Bob wants very much to know you. He lost his father when he was about your age; he was killed in an accident, and he says all that's happened has been harder on you, Jo dear, than I realized. Bob wants to teach you to sail when we come back to Ohio to live.*

Jo looked up from the letter. "Gran," he said tensely, "I don't have to go, do I? What would Rid and Quicksie do?"

"What would your grandfather and I do without you?" laughed Gran, rumpling his hair. "You will be able to do what you like," she said, suddenly serious. "Live with them and visit us, or live with us and visit them. There's a good school not too far away and the bus goes past here every morning. I'd miss you, Jo," said Gran. "I'd miss you if you went away."

Suddenly he could believe her and his heart felt very full of something he wanted to express —but couldn't.

Without stopping to think, and driven by the desire not to do any more stealing of food if he could help it, Jo blurted out, "Gran, could I have some extra sandwiches?"

His grandmother glanced at his bulging saddlebag and then looked questioningly at Jo.

The blue eyes that met hers had a desperate look in them, a look that said: "Please don't ask questions; just give me the food."

Gran remained thoughtful for a moment. When she looked up there was a strange expression of half understanding on her face.

"Jo," she asked quietly, "would you like a whole loaf of bread and a big hunk of cheese to put in your knapsack?"

"Yes!" cried Jo breathlessly.

"Wait," directed Gran. "I'll be back in a minute."

When she returned, she handed him not only a large loaf and at least a pound of cheese but a packet of dried dates as well. She looked as if she wanted to say something, opened her mouth, then closed it. Patting him on the shoulder, she finally declared, "You're a good boy, Jo."

He saw her later waving to him from the terrace. After a moment or so, as he rode off across the field, he glanced back and saw she was still watching him. "She cares where I go," he thought.

His knapsack was heavy on his back, for it held not only Quicksie's oats but the other provisions. Fastened to the saddle was his sandwich bag.

Tony did not come out from the cabin to greet him, and Jo tensed with apprehension. "They've gotten him—they found him," he thought with dismay. Then this reaction was followed by a sense of selfish relief.

But supposing it were himself? He began to worry again about Tony, and with all haste he unsaddled Quicksie and turned her out in the corral. "I'll get your water in a minute," he said. As he glanced at the sky he saw it was becoming more and more threatening.

There was a strange silence about the cabin as Jo pushed the groaning, squeaking door.

Quickly his eyes searched the seemingly empty room until they lighted on a pathetic figure bundled in a blanket and crouched on the rough bed. A black mane of hair stuck up over the edge of the blanket.

"Tony!" called Jo anxiously.

A moan answered him, and Jo strode across

157

the cabin and pulled back an edge of the cover.

"What's the matter?" he asked.

Tony's face was a mass of little blister-like spots.

"Look at me," he said, and pointed to his arms which were covered too. "I think I got smallpox —I'm going to die!" And he scratched and thrashed about on the bunk.

Jo was appalled. "I brought you a lot of food, Tony," he said tentatively. "Here's some cheese. See, it says *Genuine Imported Switzerland Swiss* on the cover. I'll bet it's good."

To Jo's amazement the dying invalid showed great interest and ate a very thick cheese sandwich Jo prepared.

"Sit down and talk to me," begged Tony pleadingly. "It's awful lonesome here alone. Hi, Rid," he said to the dog, who had just trotted in the door and accepted him with a glance. "Say, do you know the day you found me I thought your dog was a bloodhound when I heard him sniffing around the cabin. I thought

158

the cops had found me for sure."

Jo sat down on a three-legged wooden stool beside the bunk and Rid put his head on Jo's knee. "Hello, you fierce bloodhound," he said, and gently pulled the dog's ears sideways so they stood out like sails.

"Gosh, he looks funny." Tony laughed and pulled an arm out of the blanket to point at the dog.

Jo looked speculatively at Tony. "I'll bet your stepfather made you awful mad when he was beating up your mother."

"Yeah," said Tony, "he sure did. They say I should have called the cops instead of hitting him with a chair." His voice was very low as he added, "But he might have hurt her before I could have found a cop. He had no business to lay a hand on her. He'd been drinking again."

Jo didn't say anything; he gnawed on a hang-nail and looked at Tony.

"Just as soon as I get out of reform school I'm going to start working to earn money for

Ma. I wonder how she and the kids are getting on." Tony went into a paroxysm of scratching and began to moan.

"I didn't mean to kill him!" His black haunted eyes seemed to be pleading with Jo for understanding. "I just wanted to make him stop what he was doing. And now I've run away and I'll probably have to do more time when they catch me."

"Yes," said Jo, "I know."

Thunder was muttering over the hills and a lightning flash lit up the cabin window. The gathering storm made the room dusky. Tony's splotched white face was in deep shadow, his shoulders were slumped under the rough blanket and his legs, in their wrinkled brown pants ending in scuffed shoes, stuck out over the edge of the bunk toward Jo. "Say," he asked suddenly, "are you Catholic?"

"No," said Jo. He felt rather embarrassed because his family didn't go to church at all. They'd sent him to Sunday School one winter but he didn't know what he was. Nothing, probably.

"Ever heard of St. Patrick's Cathedral?" asked Tony.

"No," said Jo. "What's that?"

Tony gloried in a momentary feeling of superiority.

"Well, it's a great big church, the biggest church in New York."

Jo didn't know and he assumed an air of indifference.

But Tony had had an experience and he was going to tell about it. "Some guy said to me, 'If you light a candle at the cathedral, what you pray for will come true.' "

"I'll bet you didn't believe that," said Jo.

"Well sure, I did believe it," said Tony, and a bitter look came over his face. "There's a guy, he sometimes gives me a quarter for running an errand for him and I have fifty cents, see, so I walk and I take a bus to this great big church— it's way up on Fifth Avenue."

Jo looked blank and Tony went on. "I never seen nothing like that church, it was so big it made you feel kind of small, you know." He paused. "Kind of like these woods around here," he said, suddenly astonished.

Jo's face registered a sort of comprehension and Tony went on.

"I light a candle; boy, there was more candles than I ever seen, sort of a pond like of little flames, you know."

Jo thought of the sun on the water and nodded.

Tony scratched at his spotted face and went on. "Well, like I said, I light this candle and I pray that this guy that's married to my mother won't do her no more harm." A harsh look of disillusionment made his mouth twist down. "Well, it was that night he started to beat her up again, and I hit him."

Jo tipped back and forth a couple of times on his stool. Suddenly he looked at Tony. "Well, he's not beating her up any more, is he?" he asked practically.

A stupid look of wonder came over Tony's pale face. "Gee," he said, "he's not, is he?"

They fell into a moody silence, listening to the muttering thunder which was drawing closer.

Jo got up from the stool. "If you're eighteen

they hang people for murder in England," he said.

Tony shrank down into his blanket like an animal retreating into a hole. "Here you burn," he whispered.

Jo moved uneasily. "I'd better get Quicksie some water. We really should go home before the storm."

"You'll never beat this storm!" declared Tony. "It's coming any minute now."

Jo saw that Tony was right. As he dipped up a bucketful of water from the pond he glanced up at black clouds billowing toward him like oily smoke.

The mare drank a little water but she seemed rather nervous. She raised her head and blew through her nose. The rising wind whipped her mane and tail. Jo patted her encouragingly and then returned to the cabin carrying the saddle and bridle.

"Night's going to come early with this storm," said Tony. "I found a candle and some matches in a box. I haven't never used the candle because

I always go to sleep when it gets dark. I sleep a lot—there's nothing else to do."

"Don't you ever go rowing in the boat?" asked Jo.

"No, I don't know how and I'm scared of drowning if I fell out. Besides, Bill the Butch and Harold might be prowling around in the woods and see me. Gosh, I can't stand this itching!" he exclaimed, and began again to thrash about on the bunk. "It's driving me nuts, you've no idea. I bet I'm going to die," he said again miserably.

"Oh, I don't think so," Jo encouraged him. "Hey, how were the potatoes?" he inquired eagerly.

"Kind of raw," said Tony, "but I ate them."

Jo, who had hoped for a better report on his first venture in cooking, was crestfallen but suddenly he remembered something he had saved up to tell Tony.

"Did you hear about those dolphins?" he asked. "They're as smart as humans. The Navy is doing experiments with them. I saw about it in the newspapers. Those things can talk to each other in dolphin language and they try to speak English. When they try, it sounds sort of like Donald Duck."

Tony moaned; he was too miserable to be really interested.

Outside, the rising wind whipped branches against the cabin.

"It's true," persisted Jo. "The Navy says they have brains as good as humans. I want to have a dolphin for a pet and teach it English. Then I would get it to explore for treasure in old sunken ships on the bottom of the ocean. I'd buy a diving suit and my dolphin would show me where the treasure is and I'd be rich."

"Jo, I can't stand this!" cried Tony. "Can't you do something?"

A terrific flash of lightning was followed almost at once by a pistol crack of thunder. Both boys and Rid started with fright. The dog tried to creep under Jo's stool. In the ensuing silence Jo heard Quicksie neigh. She's afraid too, he thought. I've got to go to her.

The wind, which had paused as if shocked into quiet by the terrible thunder crash, rose again and the first great pattering drops of rain hit the cabin window.

In Jo's fast-beating heart a resolve was forming, and he jumped to his feet and measured the big cabin door with his eye.

"I'm going to bring Quicksie in here!" he cried.

"No!" squeaked Tony. "I'm afraid of horses."

"I'm going to, anyway," called Jo defiantly, as he flung open the door and rushed out. The rain pelted him, almost blinding him, and plastered his hair down over his forehead as he raced toward the corral.

He could see the mare standing facing him in the murky light. Water streamed from her darkened coat. Her ears were flattened back in protest at the roaring of the wind in the trees and the feel of the pelting rain.

"Oh, God, don't let another of those thunders come before I get her in!" prayed Jo.

As he let down the bars of the corral, a flash silhouetted the horse against the tossing trees, and before he could count three the thunder clapped again. Jo didn't need to whistle, the

166

mare came straight to him. "She has no halter. How am I going to lead her?" he thought desperately.

He mustn't panic, he mustn't hurry too much or she'd catch fright from him and be hard to handle. "She's been out in rain before," he thought. "Maybe she doesn't mind it as much as I do. She doesn't know you can get struck by lightning."

Oh, to be back in the cabin! But he couldn't leave her alone in the storm. Forcing himself to move slowly, he wound his right hand into her mane as he stood on her near side and put his left hand across her nose.

"Come on, Quicksie," he said shakily, and started to walk.

Flash! Crack! The storm struck again, and the whole pond and the cabin were illumined and then sank back into dimness. The mare was easy to handle. She took the whole thing more calmly than Jo, but as they came up to the cabin she stopped dead in her tracks. She just wouldn't move when he tried to walk her toward the door.

"Come on, Quicksie. Come on, girl!" cried

Jo, his teeth chattering with fright and wetness. But she wouldn't move. Again the thunder and lightning struck, and the rain came down as if all heaven's hydrants were opened.

"Come, Quicksie," urged Jo again desperately. "It's just like your stable; you go into your stall every night, you know." He tried to pull her by her mane toward the cabin.

Inside the open door he could dimly see Tony wrapped in his blanket, crouched in frozen terror in a corner of the bunk. Rid was still using the stool to shield his head from the sounds of the storm. He didn't like noise and his hanging tail was a measure of his low spirits.

Jo was debating whether to try to lead the mare back to the corral. Once more he urged her to move.

"You whinnied; you said you were lonesome. Now come on inside," he pleaded.

In one of those lulls which always occur in storms, when the rain lets up and everything seems to be waiting for the next terrible flash and crack, Jo called to his dog.

"Rid! Rid!" he cried. He didn't have much idea of how the dog could help, but he knew Tony would be of no use at all.

Obeying the sound of his master's voice, Rid pulled his head out from under the stool and came to Jo, tail and ears drooping miserably.

Quicksie's ears pricked forward as she recognized her friend, who almost immediately retreated into the cabin and sat on the floor facing the door and the pouring rain. His sagging ears and mournful expression seemed to say that he wouldn't venture out into that storm again for anyone.

Jo tugged at the mare's mane once more and tentatively she moved slowly forward, head lowered to keep her eyes on the dog. With Jo following her and patting her flank, she walked right into the cabin. Rid licked her on the nose and probably told her in animal language that she was mighty lucky to be inside.

Jo closed the door with a bang and bolted it against the raging storm. He heard Tony mumbling feebly in his corner. He apparently didn't dare talk out loud for fear of attracting the horse's attention and being eaten alive. Jo rather thought Tony was praying to be saved.

"Thinks he's Daniel in the lions' den," Jo chuckled to himself.

"It's all right, Tony," he called heartily. "She's as gentle as a kitten. Listen," he continued, "the Arabs always bring their horses into their tents at night. Arab chieftains lie down beside their horses to sleep."

"Is this one going to lie down?" croaked Tony.

"I don't know," said Jo, "maybe not. Horses can sleep standing up, you see. I must dry her off so she won't catch cold." He glanced around the cabin looking for a rag and his eyes fell on Tony's blanket.

"No," said Tony firmly and wrapped it tighter than ever around himself. "Here I am, probably dying, and you just looked at my blanket as if you wanted to take it away and use it on an old horse. There's a couple of sacks in that box by the window," he advised grudgingly.

With the rough burlap sacks Jo began going

170

over the mare, rubbing her down over and over until she was almost dry. His arms were aching and he finally paused and patted her neck.

"I'll give you your oats," he decided, and he shook them out of the knapsack into a deep frying pan which he set on the floor in front of her. The mare eagerly scooped up the oats with her soft lips and, when they were eaten, moved her head over the earth floor looking for spilled grains.

As the afternoon wore on, the thunder went muttering off over the hills, but the rain continued.

"I should start home," said Jo, rising and going to the window.

"No, no!" cried Tony piteously. "You can't leave me to die alone. I'd rather spend the night with a horse than all alone."

Jo really felt for him. He could see Tony wasn't fooling, that he had had about all he could take.

"But they'll wonder where I am," Jo protested feebly. Then he remembered having heard his grandmother and grandfather say they were going out to supper. They had probably started by now, expecting that he'd make for home when the worst of the storm had passed. Undoubtedly Freedle would tell them when they returned that evening that he hadn't come in. He was afraid they would worry.

"I must go," he said.

As if nature were on the side of poor frightened Tony, the storm which had retreated began to return. A vivid flash of lightning lit the cabin window and thunder reverberated over the hills. Jo saw the leaves of the great oaks by the corral lit with an eerie green light. He had no desire to go outside.

There was a coziness inside the cabin which now smelled of horse, wet dog and mustiness. Everyone had gotten used to everyone else. Jo hadn't wanted to light a fire because Gramp had said that horses are instinctively afraid of fire. Anyway, they really didn't need it. Jo had become pretty well dried off during his exertions in rubbing down the mare.

172

"Let's eat," said Jo, "I'm hungry." He had lunched with Tony on only bread and cheese, and now he reached for the sandwich bag on his saddle, which lay in a corner by the fireplace.

Between scratches Tony watched with interest as Jo unpacked the provisions. There were lettuce, bacon and tomato sandwiches, sardine sandwiches, chicken sandwiches and spice cake. Freedle had included a couple of apples and a carrot, which Jo set aside for Quicksie.

Rid, who had tentatively stuck his head back under the stool at the first roll of thunder, pulled it out when he smelled the chicken sandwiches and began to pant with anticipation.

Keeping his eye on the horse, Tony ventured far enough from his bed to get the candle, which he stuck in an old bottle and set lighted on the window sill.

They were a cheerful party as they gathered round the supper spread out on the bunk. Now the occasional flashes of lightning and rolls of thunder only made the cabin seem cozier and safer. A calm, steady rain drummed on the roof.

Quicksie had finished her oats and moved around so her head was beside Jo's as he sat on the stool. Rid was in his usual mealtime-begging position, his eyes riveted on the chicken sandwiches. Even Tony seemed to forget his awful itching momentarily as he crouched in a corner of the bunk, but he still kept away from the animals.

"I'm going to give Rid a couple of the chicken sandwiches," said Jo firmly. "If he's hungry he'll eat the bread." He broke one in half to make it last longer and offered it to the dog. Rid this time was hungry enough to eat both bread and meat in a gulp.

Tony, seeing his favorite food being handed to Rid, snatched at a sandwich and began to eat, watching curiously as Jo fed the dog before he began on his own supper. Thinking of animals before yourself was a new idea to Tony.

"Hey," said Jo looking reprovingly at him, "go slow on the chicken sandwiches. Rid likes them."

"Rid likes them," mimicked Tony. "Well, so do I. He's only a dog, ain't he?"

The thunder was moving closer again; it shook the hills. Night had come on by now and the only light in the cabin was that of the candle. Wavering shadows of horse, dog, and boys danced on the rough walls as the candle flared in the draft from a window crack.

Jo reached over his shoulder to feed Quicksie a carrot, and the sound of sharp crunching filled the little room.

"Have an apple," he suggested as the mare nudged his shoulder for more.

Tony watched with interest. "Here's another one for her," he said, picking up the last apple and handing it to Jo. It obviously fascinated him to watch a horse eat.

"Want a piece of sardine sandwich, Rid?" Jo asked, but the dog, after one sniff, rejected it and gazed soulfully again at the remains of the chicken sandwich. Jo finally gave it to him.

Jo, who usually didn't like fish, was glad to eat the sardines.

"You'd better sleep on the bunk with me," said Tony, "unless you're afraid of catching the smallpox."

Jo had opened his mouth to reply when a furious flash of lightning lit the room. Simultaneously a tearing, snarling rip of thunder tore the heavens apart. Quicksie reared up, Rid began to whine, Tony cried out. Only Jo was silent—but shaking.

"It struck right by us," whimpered Tony and, as if his words had brought the thing to pass, a cracking, rushing, thundering noise left them breathless.

Jo jumped up and put a hand on Quicksie's neck.

"Steady, girl, it's all right now." He felt the sweat of fear on her and forgot his own terror as he tried to calm his horse.

"A tree came down," he said shakily to Tony. "The lightning struck it." They all stood listening, dreading another thunder clap. But it was as if the storm had wreaked its final vengeance, for it growled off into the hills like a beast.

Jo went to the window. Lightning flickered once more, and to his horror he saw that the giant oak had fallen straight across Quicksie's corral. For a moment he couldn't even speak, then he turned toward Tony.

"If she'd been out there she would have been killed," he said, his voice shaking.

"Who?" asked Tony.

"Quicksie," said Jo. "That tree went down right where she would have been standing."

"Wow!" exclaimed Tony, much impressed. "It might have happened while you was out there, Jo, and then what would have become of me?"

"What would have become of me?" thought Jo. But aloud he said, "We'd better try to get some sleep. Move over on that bunk and Rid can lie between us."

"You're sure he won't bite me?" asked Tony.

"I promise he won't," said Jo. "He sort of likes you now I think."

"I guess you would have caught the smallpox by now if you was going to," said Tony philosophically, and he moved over against the wall. Jo pulled an end of the blanket over himself and Rid.

"I'll just sleep a little while," he thought. "I must start for home as soon as there's any light."

## II

Toward dawn Jo awoke. It was pitch dark and still, except for the sound of dripping from the cabin eaves. He heard Tony moan and felt the blanket jerk as he scratched himself in his sleep. The room smelled strongly of horse, and as Jo listened he heard Quicksie shift her weight where she stood on the earth floor and heard the gentle whiffling she made through her nose.

It seemed that it was about four o'clock in the

morning, for the air had that special feeling that comes just before dawn. Jo lay there thinking. Tony had told him to "do something." Did that mean Tony was prepared to give himself up and take the consequences? Jo hoped so. "I'll try to get his permission to tell Gramp. He'll know what we should do."

An enormous feeling of relief surged over Jo now that he had thought out a way to lay the problem on Gramp's shoulders without betraying Tony. He was sure that in his heart Tony knew he couldn't stay here forever and knew that he had had nearly enough of living alone in the woods. "He must be scared though of what they'll do to him once they get him back at that reform school," thought Jo, "but I guess right now he feels too awful to care."

"Tony's not bad," Jo reasoned. "After all, he *was* trying to save his mother. Maybe Gramp will be able to help him some way." He hoped Tony would get over his awful disease.

Suddenly an idea, which he had been too tired to consider last night, hit him with a sickening

179

jolt. Supposing Tony really did have smallpox and he caught it from him—would he die? The thought of Gran catching it from him made him wince. To think of Gran covered all over with spots and his having given them to her was intolerable. These thoughts made him admit to himself that he loved his grandmother dearly.

Beside him Rid stirred and then settled closer, giving a great sigh of comfort and security.

Above the faint drip, drip from the eaves Jo heard the sleepy note of a waking bird, then another joined in. Looking toward the window he saw the pane was not quite pitch black.

"I should get up," he thought. "Gran and Gramp must wonder where I am." A happy feeling came over him. Instead of brooding about being the boy nobody wanted, he began to count all those who needed him—Quicksie, Rid, Tony, Gran and Gramp—even his mother. He could think of his mother now and be glad she was happy. She wanted him and so did Bob. Maybe even his father thought about him sometimes, who could tell? Perhaps he'd see him again some day. He remembered the big case of soft drinks his father had given him on his birthday. He'd known Jo wanted it and so he'd given it to him. "That *was* nice, wasn't it?" thought Jo. "He wanted me to be happy, didn't he?"

Bird voices began to swell into a chorus of songs; there was light enough now to see Quicksie. Head up, ears pricked, she was looking toward the window, greeting the dawn.

"She must be hungry and thirsty," thought Jo. At home she would have had a big pile of hay in her stall during the night. He wondered what he could give her; all the oats were gone. There was some grass in the clearing near the pond but it would be awfully wet after last night's rain.

He knew she shouldn't have too much wet grass if she was hungry because she would bolt it, but a little would be all right. What could he use to lead her with? If he let her loose she would surely make for home and oats. An inspiration came to him—he'd make a halter by taking the bit out of her bridle and use a rein as a lead rope.

Softly, so as not to disturb Tony, he crept out

of bed. Rid sat up, then jumped to the floor and shook himself. Tony slept on.

Working carefully, he slipped the makeshift halter over the mare's ears. She was eager to go and turned around, noisily clumping on the earth floor.

"You ain't leaving?" mumbled Tony.

"I'll be back in a minute," Jo assured him. "I'm just going to let my horse get some breakfast. You stay there."

Jo opened the big creaking door and led the mare out into the dawn light. Before him water lay drenched in mist that moved in drifts like smoke.

"Ghostly Pond!" thought Jo. "That's how Gramp must have seen it too. Now I know why he named the pond; I never understood before."

The mare lowered her head to crop the fresh wet grass. She wrenched her head sideways to get big bites and kept strolling toward the water. "I'll let her drink from the pond where there's a shallow place to the right," he thought, and he guided her gently as she ate.

182

Lying just beneath the ripples at the water's edge he saw a blue stone shaped like a bird's egg. He thought it very pretty and picking it up, put it in his pocket. "I'll give it to Gran," he said to himself.

The mare drank then raised her head with water dripping from her lips, and pricked her ears toward the east where the sky was beginning to glow red through the trees. With head raised high she looked joyfully into the coming

day and whinnied as if she saw some spirit horse in the mists over the water.

"I'll tell Gramp I've seen his ghosts," Jo promised himself. "But why doesn't he come over often to Ghostly Pond?" He had half forgotten what Gramp had told him. Oh, yes, three leaves and shiny; there was some of it right at his feet —poison ivy—POISON IVY! He gave a great whoop.

"Hey, Tony. Tony!" he called.

The mare started at his sudden shout, and he laid a hand on her neck.

Hearing Jo yell, Tony was sure he was being warned that a boatload of police were rowing across the pond so he ducked under the blanket and lay still as a mouse.

With the lead strap in his hand, Jo ran toward the cabin and Quicksie trotted along shaking her head. Rid, who had been taking an early morning bath, came galumphing out of the shallows splashing water in all directions and ran after them to see what was up.

"Tony. Hey, Tony!" cried Jo. "Don't be

scared. I didn't yell 'Fourth of July'—it's just
that I know what's the matter with you."

"What?" asked Tony, whose black shock of
hair and speckled face peeked out from the
blanket.

"You've got poison ivy!" cried Jo.

"Poison what?" squeaked Tony, his eyes big
with fright. Poison ivy doesn't grow in New York
City and Tony had never heard of it. But the
word POISON was understandable enough. He
had seen deaths'-heads and crossed bones on
bottles and had read in the paper of people who
had died because they had drunk poison, so Jo's
triumphant shout didn't do anything but increase
his anxiety.

"Look, Tony," said Jo, seeing that his ex-
planation wasn't getting anywhere, "do you remember touching a sort of plant with three shiny
leaves growing on one stem?"

"Aw, I don't know," said Tony. "The first
day I come here I took a sleep lying in some sort
of green stuff with leaves."

"That was poison ivy!" cried Jo. "It's all over

the place but I don't seem to be allergic to it. Anyway, I know what it looks like and sort of watch out for it. You'll get over it in a few days," he added, "and a doctor can give you some medicine so it won't itch so much."

"Oh, yeah?" asked Tony wonderingly.

"I didn't think you were very sick the way you've been eating," said Jo.

"What's for breakfast?" asked Tony. "Cheese?"

"There are some dates and we could eat bread," answered Jo. "Get a move on and fill me a cup of water at the spring. I've got to let my horse eat. You're not sick," he added. "You just itch and you were scared."

"You're sure I'm not going to die?" asked Tony hopefully, returning from the spring with the brimful cups.

"No, of course you're not going to die. But I think you should see a doctor," he added hastily. Jo suddenly began to wonder whether Tony was going to decide to keep on hiding. "You really should see a doctor," he said again. "You've

scratched so much maybe you're sort of infected."

"Infected?" Tony looked worried once more.
"You know, Jo, I've decided that if I'm going to
ever begin earning money for my Ma I got to
serve out my sentence. I got to give myself up."

Jo didn't want to show how immensely relieved he felt. "Look, Tony, my grandfather is
sort of an important man." (Jo didn't know just
what he meant by this except he felt that Gramp
would be able to make things come right.) "You
wait. He'll see they don't beat you up or anything," he added a bit lamely.

Tony had found the dates. "Give me a few,"
said Jo.

The sun was showing a rim of gold and was
being encouraged to rise by a chorus of every
bird in the woods.

"Hand me my saddle, Tony," said Jo presently. "The bit's lying beside it; get that too."

Yesterday afternoon Tony wouldn't any
more have dared come close to Quicksie than to
a tiger in the zoo. But now, having eaten supper

with her and then slept in the same room, he regarded her almost as a friend. He passed Jo the bit and held the saddle until he was ready to put it on.

As Jo fastened the girth, Tony stood with his hand rather timidly on the mare's neck.

"Are you going to get your grandfather to help me?" asked Tony.

"Do you want me to?" asked Jo.

"Yeah," answered Tony.

"Don't you worry, Tony," advised Jo as he gathered up the reins and mounted while Rid jumped about, ready to go. "Everything will be all right"—he hoped.

"So long," he added. "We'll be back," and he started along the path.

Before he disappeared around the clump of pine trees, he turned and waved at the spotty, forlorn figure standing by the cabin door.

# 12

It must be about seven o'clock, thought Jo. Gran and Gramp will be getting up in half an hour. Jo was worried. He had ridden almost all the way home at a canter but had walked the last half mile or so to bring his horse in cool. Now she was bedded down in her stall with a full water bucket, a manger of oats and a good pile of hay.

He hastened toward the house, half expecting to see his grandparents out looking for him. He was sure that they must have been worried when Freedle told them that he hadn't returned for supper. It would soon be time for her to bong on the rising gong—he'd better hurry.

He noticed a strange stillness about the place as he approached the great vine-covered house. The sheep grazed placidly on the lawn under the big trees. But there were no sounds of breakfast preparations coming from the kitchen door. He went in followed by Rid and walked through the empty room where a ticking alarm clock on top of the stove pointed to quarter before seven. There was no sign of the table being set in the dining room. He went upstairs quietly, half afraid that the house was empty except for himself and his dog.

He needed to visit the bathroom near his room and after that he was going to knock on Gran and Gramp's door whether it was time for them to get up or not. He felt very uneasy.

His feet and Rid's thudded softly on the matting as they went along the upstairs passage. But when they came to the door of the unused sitting room he was brought to a halt by a strange moaning cry. Jo turned pale. He remembered the night weeks ago when he had first walked down this corridor and how Freedle had paused and listened.

"In this room comes the ghost," she had whispered.

"Rid, listen!" implored Jo. The crying moan came again. Rid looked up at Jo and wagged his tail.

With the dog beside him to give him courage, Jo opened the door a crack and peeped in. A strong scent of violets was blown toward him. The window was open and curtains fluttered in the early morning breeze. Rid was whining eagerly. All at once Jo saw the blue rug in front of a bookcase begin to bump up and down in a most mystifying way. His mouth dropped open and he hung on to the doorknob for support, but Rid ran forward, tail wagging.

"He's not afraid of ghosts," thought Jo. "Gosh, I wouldn't go in there for anything. Come here, Rid!" he called. He wanted to get out of there and close the door and run to get Gran and Gramp—if he could find them. But he wouldn't leave his dog behind at the mercy of this strange spirit that showed its presence by bumping a rug up and down.

"Come here, Rid!" he called desperately. The dog looked back at him and his eyes were gay and laughing; he wagged his tail harder than ever.

Just then Jo heard the moaning cry once more. Something familiar about it made him forget his fear and move into the room. He grasped the edge of the rug and found it nailed on to cover a trap door. Using a lot of strength, for it was heavy, he flung the lid back with a bump.

Rid's tail-wagging became even more enthusiastic as Jo peered into the gaping hole. At first Jo thought he had found a golden treasure as he leaned over the hole and peered down. But the gold suddenly tipped backwards and a very pink and angry face was turned up to him. A hand reached out clasping an empty perfume bottle that reeked of violets.

"Freedle Popinpoose! You are the ghost!" cried Jo.

"Well, do something," moaned the ghost. "I'm stuck."

"What's the big idea?" exclaimed Jo. First he was mad at having been so scared and then he wanted to laugh. Freedle looked like a fat lady Santa Claus stuck halfway down a chimney.

"You get me loose and I tell you all about it," Freedle wailed, puffing with fury at her predicament.

"Are you standing on steps?" asked Jo.

"Ya," assented Freedle. "You push on my shoulders, and maybe I start down."

Jo knelt, and putting his hands on her shoulders, he pressed down all his weight. Suddenly, like a cork pushed down into a bottle, Freedle descended a couple of steps with a rush and a loud sigh of relief.

"Pull the door down and come after me," called up Freedle. "I show you something."

Rid had already shot down the little stairs after her disappearing form. To him, Freedle meant food and he was hungry after his night out.

Jo tugged at the trap door and brought it back up into a vertical position; then, holding it with a heavy hook screwed on the underside, he started down the dark little staircase one step at a time. He let the lid close gradually as he descended until it bumped tight and all the daylight from the top was shut out. Glancing down, he saw the glimmer of a light that guided the last part of his descent.

As his feet met solid ground he looked about to try to find out where he was. His descent had ended in a cupboard, the door of which was open, and through it he could see mops and brooms, cans of tomatoes, and other supplies on shelves. Why, this was the storeroom off the kitchen!

"See!" exclaimed Freedle who was standing in the middle of the kitchen floor. "I tell you I show you something. Secret staircase!"

"But why don't Gran and Gramp know about it?" asked Jo.

"Sit down," commanded Freedle. "I tell you all." And she began to busy herself with preparing breakfast while she talked.

"Like I told you when you come here, Mr. and Mrs. Shaw never bother with the practical things like cooking and cleaning. They leave it all to me," declared Freedle proudly.

"It's like this. One day I'm putting away cans of tomatoes and pretty soon I find the shelf full —I need more space. In the storeroom there's a big cupboard but the door's nailed shut. I get some tools and pretty soon I open it but I am disappointed. No shelves—stairs. So I say, 'let's see where the stairs go,' and I find out.

"Then one day your grandfather is talking at supper about ghosts. He likes ghosts—he named that pond after ghosts. I like your grandfather, your grandfather likes ghosts, so I say to myself, 'I make Mr. Shaw a ghost.' Then I wonder what kind of a ghost will I make. But just right after that I hear Mr. and Mrs. Shaw talking one night at supper about a letter she'd found in the attic. It tells about a nice girl who gets violets and she waves good-by and her soldier gets killed. Then she dies, broken heart or maybe it was the measles—I forget which," said Freedle, who had finished pouring orange juice into glasses.

" 'Aha, I have a ghost,' I say to myself, and I buy some perfume that smells like the bouquet the poor soldier boy gave his girl.

"So you see, I make Mr. Shaw happy," finished Freedle proudly.

"Do you suppose he really believed it was a ghost?" asked Jo.

"Believe it!" exclaimed Freedle in a shocked

196

voice. "And me spending my money on expensive violet perfume just to please him! Of course he believed it." With that she banged the coffee pot down onto the stove.

Jo wasn't at all certain. He was sure his grandfather had enjoyed the whole thing anyway.

"I've got to go and wash up for breakfast. Let me bong the gong to wake them up will you, Freedle?"

"Well, just this once," conceded Freedle. "I don't know whether I'm on feet or on horses," she complained, running her hand over her braids to smooth them.

"Listen, Freedle," Jo remembered something. "Didn't Gran and Gramp wonder where I was when you told them I hadn't come in for supper?"

"They never hear about that," said Freedle. "When they go off for supper the storm has stopped for a little while and they say 'if Jo doesn't come home all right you call us up and tell us.' Well, when you don't come home I think the lightning's killed you and I'd better call your grandma where they are at supper, but first I think I make a ghost so your poor grandpa have something nice to think about in the morning when he feels bad because he's lost you. Then I can't tell them because I'm stuck, and Mr. and Mrs. Shaw think right now you are asleep in your bed."

On his way upstairs Jo bonged the Chinese gong with the little mallet wrapped in cloth. Coming back from the bathroom he remembered that the window would still be wide open in the sitting room and that he had better close it.

As he came back into the passageway he met his grandfather who had wakened early and was just coming out of his room.

"There you are!" cried Gramp. "I expect you had a wet ride back yesterday afternoon," and, without waiting to hear the story Jo was bursting to tell him, he continued in one breath, "but what were you doing in the ghost room? Don't tell me the romantic young lady has been haunting these premises again."

Jo was tired of lies and evasions and Freedle hadn't asked him not to tell.

198

"Look, Gramp," said Jo, and led the way into the unused sitting room where he lifted the trap door with the rug nailed onto it.

"Well, well, well," said Gramp nodding his head up and down. "It goes into the kitchen, I presume?"

"The storeroom," answered Jo.

"Your grandmother will be relieved," said Gramp, "but—" and he sighed. "I've always felt it makes a house a home to have a ghost. Still, one must carry on in spite of life's little disappointments."

Suddenly Gramp ran his hand through his hair until it stood on end. He had thought of something pleasant.

"I sold the mare to the man we had supper with last night!" he exclaimed with an air of satisfaction.

Jo turned white and sagged against the wall.

"What's the matter, Jo?" asked Gramp, grabbing his arm and leading him downstairs into the fresh air. "Don't you feel well? Here, sit down," and he pulled forward a bench on the terrace.

Jo sat down hard then looked up at his grandfather, who was standing over him eying him with great concern. The boy's blue eyes were dark with hurt and he was barely able to speak.

"You sold Quicksie?" he mumbled.

Gramp dropped into the seat beside Jo and flung his arm across his shoulders. *"No,"* he shouted. "No! What do you think I am? It's the brown mare, the brood mare and her foal I'm talking about." He shook Jo's shoulder.

"Good heavens! Didn't I tell you I was thinking of selling her to the man we dined with last night?"

"No," said Jo weakly.

"Quicksie's yours!" cried Gramp. "How could I sell her, even if I were such a beast as to want to?"

"She's mine?" asked Jo shakily. "Really mine?"

"Yes, yours for ever and ever," said Gramp solemnly.

Jo looked up at him and Gramp turned away; the boy's eyes were too full of hurt turning into unbelievable relief and happiness. He pulled out his handkerchief and blew his nose a terrific toot.

"Don't you know," asked Gramp, "that when you make an animal really yours, you wouldn't sell it for anything? Would you sell Rid for a million dollars?" he asked.

"No," said Jo.

"Or Quicksie?" asked Gramp.

"No," said Jo.

"Why?" asked Gramp.

"Because I love them," said Jo simply.

"There you are!" exclaimed Gramp. "When a horse ceases to be just a horse and it's something you love, money doesn't count. Didn't I tell you the first night you came here that money wasn't important?"

"Yes," said Jo humbly.

Gramp started to get up from the bench.

"Oh, please wait a minute!" Jo implored. "I have something I have to tell you."

"Fine," agreed Gramp, "but I'll just bring us out a couple of plates of breakfast. It's better to talk outdoors—things never seem so bad when you're out under the sky."

# 13

As Jo's story unfolded, Gramp looked more and more serious.

"You haven't seen the papers lately, have you?" he asked. "I guess not; for we've hidden them every day because Freedle got in such a panic about a murderer being at large in the community. There have been headlines and editorials about this boy Tony. It appears people feel he didn't get a fair trial. On going over the coroner's report, it seems obvious that Tony's stepfather died of a heart attack when Tony knocked him to the floor with a chair. The neighbors have now come forward and told how badly the man treated Tony's mother. When he'd been drinking he was dangerous and everyone was afraid of him. Actually they see now that Tony was pretty brave to defend her. The authorities are ready to pardon him if he is found. Everyone thinks he must have drowned while trying to make his way along the river in the night. It's known that he didn't have any idea how to swim."

"What Tony needs right now is something to stop his poison ivy itch," said Jo.

"Oh!" exclaimed Gramp with heartfelt sympathy. "Does he have poison ivy, poor chap? I know what that can be like. There's some wonderful medicine I have left from my last bout with the filthy weed. You must take it right over to him." He jumped up. "I'll put in a phone call and let people know the boy is found."

"How can we get him out?" asked Jo. "He can't ride a horse and it would take him half a day to walk here from the cabin."

"Tom Bruckel has a jeep and there's a road

cut through his woods to bring out lumber. We'll take down the fence at the boundary line between our place and he'll be able to get through to the cabin. You wait there with Tony. Tom Bruckel won't get around until after lunch, I imagine, so ask Freedle to put up food for two. Tell her I said to give it to you, that you're meeting a friend. For heaven's sake don't tell her who the friend is or she'll drop dead!"

Gran's light step was heard crossing the corridor and she came out to where they were sitting on the terrace. At her approach they both got up.

"Jo's been harboring a fugitive from justice in the cabin," said Gramp gazing quizzically at his grandson.

Gran smiled at Jo. A quick look passed between them.

"Thanks for the cheese, Gran. It tasted great and we had some of the bread with the dates for breakfast."

"Breakfast!" exclaimed Gran. "Weren't you sleeping here last night?"

"Jo's had a pretty hair-raising night," explained Gramp. "I'll tell you all about it as soon as I put in a telephone call. Jo, you get that medicine to Tony. I know what torture that itching can be. It's in a red tube in my top bureau drawer—you'll find it," and Gramp disappeared into the house.

Gran walked with Jo into the big cool hall where roses stood in a clear glass bowl on the table which had held lilacs the night he arrived at Strawberry Hill.

"Here, Gran," said Jo reaching into his pocket. "I found you a stone." His eyes were bright at the thought of the little blue stone egg he was going to give her. Then his face fell. The stone had turned quite gray and commonplace.

"It was blue," he said, crestfallen, "it was pretty."

"I think it's a magic stone," said Gran quickly. "Let's see." And she took it from Jo's hand and dropped it into the water of the glass bowl of roses.

Once more wet, the stone turned bright blue.

"See," said Gran, "just you and I know the secret," and she gave Jo a quick kiss.

"Gran," he asked, "do you think there's a ghost at Strawberry Hill?"

"Well—" said Gran, and she looked at Jo and gave a little wink. "Your grandfather likes the idea of a ghost," she said gently.

Jo smiled at her. "Ask Gramp what's happened," he directed. "I've got to beat it and take that medicine to Tony. So long—I'll be back for supper."

He found the tube of poison ivy ointment and put it in the pocket of his blue jeans.

Quicksie was rested and glad to see Jo when he opened her stall door. He cleaned out her feet and brushed her down, then saddled up for the second time that day. He put a halter under her bridle and fastened a lead rope around her neck. He was going to have to tie her up, for the corral was filled with the branches of the fallen tree. The mare was in excellent condition from the steady exercise she had been getting over the weeks, for Jo had usually ridden her twice a day.

"Do you want to go all the way back to the pond, Rid?" asked Jo. "Or are you too tired?" But the dog, seeing his friend saddled and bridled, was quite ready to go along. It would have broken his heart to be left behind.

After going through the gate into the field they set off at a slow jog, which Jo shortly increased to a canter for he began to think of Tony and those miserable torturing itches.

He felt lighthearted and silly with relief as his body relaxed into the joyous momentum of a canter. His mind made an accompanying rhythm from the label on the cheese he had carried to the cabin yesterday—"Switzerland Swiss, Switzerland Swiss, genuine imported, Switzerland Swiss." Quicksie's hoofs striking the path beat out the rhythm.

He slowed to a walk as the stream in the woods came in sight.

Suddenly he remembered a story he had read about a dog team that had carried medicine to Nome in Alaska when an epidemic was raging; how the man and his team of dogs had braved the blizzards and the ice to reach the stricken town, and how many lives had been saved because of their heroism.

He and Quicksie were carrying medicine to Tony. He imagined he was a doctor fording rushing streams with his brave horse to reach the victims of a plague. When he and Quicksie came to the stream and went splashing through to the other side, he was disappointed that it wasn't a little deeper.

Instead of being a pilot, he thought he might study to be a doctor and he and Quicksie would ride over the countryside to help sick people. He imagined himself doing a dangerous operation by candlelight while the family of the patient stood around wringing their hands. And finally, when he had practically performed a miracle and the sick man was resting comfortably, the wife would say, "God bless you, Doctor," and Jo would say, "Don't thank me. It was my horse who brought me here through the flooded river."

He felt Quicksie had done all that. He leaned forward and patted her neck.

He had been daydreaming so much that he

was almost surprised when the cabin came in sight.

Tony was sitting on the grass in front of the door and waved as he saw them coming. His face showed his eagerness to know what his fate was going to be.

Jo drew to a halt beside him and jumped off. Looping the reins over his arm, he searched in the saddlebag for the tube of ointment.

"Here, Tony!" he cried. "Rub this all over your face and arms and the itching will stop."

"You ain't kidding?" exclaimed Tony, and began to smear the stuff from the red tube wherever the spots itched the most.

Jo kept his eyes on his face, eagerly watching for results. After a few minutes Tony gave a great sigh and said, "It works."

"I've got lots of lunch." Jo undid the saddlebag and tossed it into Tony's hands. "Wait till I tie the mare to the corral fence. I'll be back in a minute."

"How about a little row?" Jo asked when he returned. "It's shallow down to the right of the pond. I won't take you over your head."

"What did your old grandfather say?" asked Tony. He didn't care to commit himself about a boat ride.

Jo laughed. *Old* was not a word he would think of applying to Gramp. He was anxious for Tony to meet him.

"I told you everything would turn out all right," said Jo. "Gramp says people, I don't just know who, but people who count, have decided that you weren't really guilty. Your stepfather had a heart attack, you just knocked him down. It wasn't you who killed him."

"Who did kill him?" asked Tony. "God?"

"No, Tony, listen. His heart stopped. He'd had an awful lot to drink and his heart just stopped. I guess it was drinking that killed him. Anyway, it wasn't you."

"It wasn't me?" Tony sounded dazed. "Boy, Ma will be glad."

"A man named Tom Bruckel is going to drive his jeep in here after lunch and bring you out," Jo explained cheerfully.

"Out where?" asked Tony. "Will I have to go back to Black Hill Reform School?"

"Oh, no, I'm sure you won't," Jo assured him. "Gramp will have everything fixed up, you wait and see. Come on and take a row with me—I promise I won't take you where it's deep."

Tony allowed himself to be persuaded to get into the stern of the small red boat but he sat hunched up, clutching the sides with both hands.

"Just stay still," Jo cautioned him. "Don't rock the boat—there's nothing to be scared of." He stepped lightly into the middle of the skiff and sitting down, unshipped the oars and began to row with short firm strokes, going more or less in a circle so as not to get out of shallow water.

Pretty soon Tony's face, all dabbed with white ointment over red blotches, began to fill with pleasure.

"Boy, this is great!" he said and hung one hand over the side so his fingers trailed in the water.

"Let's have some lunch," said Jo finally. He was tired of going around in a circle. "I think

I'll just take a quick swim first," he added.

When Jo came dripping out of the water a little while later, Tony was spreading the sandwiches out on a flat rock and Rid was exercising great control by sitting far enough away so as not to be too tempted. Jo didn't think Tony had eaten any this time.

It was a real feast they all enjoyed. Perhaps Freedle had been feeling grateful to Jo for having gotten her out of her tight spot, but anyway it was the best picnic lunch either of them had ever eaten. Jo was sure Freedle knew Rid's weakness for chicken sandwiches, and she had included some of those as well as a carrot for Quicksie. He must remember to thank her for everything.

When the sandwiches, the stuffed eggs, the plums, and the gingerbread cakes were eaten, they pushed the crumbs into a little heap for the birds. Jo eased back against a tree trunk to take a rest while Tony applied more ointment to his arms.

"I kind of wish Quicksie had eaten with us too, like she did last night," said Tony.

"Want to feed her a carrot?" asked Jo, and he pulled one out of his pocket.

Tony was just opening his mouth to say yes when the sound of an approaching vehicle made them both spring to their feet.

A jeep came bumping into the clearing and stopped near them. A big lanky man wearing a Stetson hat untangled his legs and climbed from under the wheel.

"I'm Tom Bruckel, Tony," he said. "Mr. Shaw asked me to come in to bring you out. He doesn't come here himself if he can help it because of the poison ivy. I see you have a dose of it yourself," and he grinned at Tony.

"I'm the probation officer around these parts," he went on, "and it's been arranged that you're to stay with me until everything gets settled up. My wife is glad to have you visit us. She's getting a big steak dinner ready and wants to know what kind of ice cream you like."

Tony was not a very prepossessing sight with his spotty white-daubed face and his long, matted black hair, but you would have thought Tom Bruckel was his best friend the way he held out his hand to Tony and helped him into the jeep.

"So long, Tony," said Jo.

"So long—I'll see you," answered Tony.

Tom Bruckel waved. "You've got your own transportation, haven't you?" he said, and threw the jeep into reverse.

As they drove off Jo saw Tony gesturing toward the fallen tree, apparently explaining what had happened. He didn't like to look at the thing himself. It made him shiver.

The chugging of the jeep died away. Suddenly it seemed very quiet there by the pond. Jo felt let down, as if something had gone out of his life. It was a funny thing. Everything had begun to go right after he found Tony. He wondered why.

"Come on, Rid, it's time to go home," he said, and ran his hand through his hair.

As they came out on the level meadow near Strawberry Hill, he crouched low on the mare's neck. "Let's go!" he cried and Quicksie, catching his excitement, broke into a canter, then a gallop, then raced flat out. He heard and felt her hoofs drumming like pistons and he saw the meadow go by in a blur of speed.

"She's as fast as a rocket and she's mine," thought Jo.

Panting with excitement, he leaned back and eased her to a stop. Then, turning her, he patted her damp neck and smoothed her dark mane while together they watched Rid trying to catch up. Paws thudding, ears flying, mouth open and tongue lolling, he sped along, doggedly determined not to be left behind.

Quicksie lowered her head to him and before he sank panting on the grass, he gave her a friendly bump on the nose. Lying at her feet, Rid looked up adoringly at Jo.

"We three," he seemed to say.